NINA

was born in London in 1925 [...] the war. She was educated at [...] and at Somerville College, Oxford.

Her first novel, *Who Calls the Tune*, appeared in 1953. Since then she has published nineteen other adult novels including: *Tortoise by Candlelight* (1963); *A Little Love, A Little Learning* (1965); *A Woman of My Age* (1967), *The Grain of Truth* (1968); *The Birds on the Trees* (1970); *Afternoon of a Good Woman*, winner of the Yorkshire Post Novel of the Year Award for 1976; *Familiar Passions* (1979); *Walking Naked* (1981); *The Ice House* (1983) and *Circles of Deceit*, which was shortlisted for the Booker Prize in 1988 and filmed by the BBC. Her most recent novel is *Family Money* (1991).

Nina Bawden is also an acclaimed author of seventeen children's books. Many of these have been televised or filmed; all have been widely translated. Amongst them are: *Carrie's War* (1973); *The Peppermint Pig*, the recipient of the 1975 Guardian Award for Children's Fiction; *The Finding* (1985), *Keeping Henry* (1988), *The Outside Child* (1989), *Humbug* (1992) and *The Real Plato Jones* (1994).

For ten years Nina Bawden served as a magistrate, both in her local court and in the Crown Court. She also sat on the councils of various literary bodies, including the Royal Society of Literature – of which she is a Fellow – PEN, and the Society of Authors, and is the President of the Society of Women Writers and Journalists. In addition she has lectured at conferences and universities, on Arts Council tours and in schools.

Nina Bawden has been married twice and has one son, one daughter and two stepdaughters. She lives in London and in Greece.

Virago publish ten of Nina Bawden's works of fiction and will publish her Autobiography, *In My Own Time* in October 1994.

VIRAGO
MODERN
CLASSIC

NUMBER
396

Nina Bawden

GEORGE BENEATH A PAPER MOON

Published by VIRAGO PRESS Limited August 1994
The Rotunda
42–43 Gloucester Crescent
London NW1 7PD

First published in Great Britain by Allen Lane, 1974
Copyright © Nina Bawden 1974

A CIP catalogue record for this book is available from the British
Library

Printed in Great Britain by Cox & Wyman Ltd, Reading Berkshire

For Canan

Chapter 1

Sometimes George felt that nothing real had ever happened to him. The world swept on its passionate and catastrophic way and he stood on the edge of it, watching.

Not that it mattered. How could it matter what happened – or didn't happen – to him? That he should get up every morning looking forward to the day seemed not only frivolous (in the face of earthquakes, wars, the population explosion) but almost impossible. The co-existence of his small, eager life and the great, burning world, was impossible.

And yet he went on with it. Slept sound at night, woke happy and hopeful, showered and shaved, put the coffee on, turned on the radio. News of enormous, incredible events came to him at the flick of a switch, while he ate eggs and bacon. His appetite seldom faltered – his body, that intricate, fragile machine, had its own innocent logic – but often his mind froze, amazed. *Here I sit, eating breakfast!*

His best friend, Sam Catto, said, 'Since Marconi invented the wireless, old boy, it's been hard for anyone to take themselves seriously.'

Sam had always managed it, though. While George hovered above the abyss like an irresolute bird, uncertain which way to fly, Sam saw what he wanted, believed it important, and shot straight towards it, hard as a bullet. He wasn't brutal – George had no brutal friends – but he had a certain civilized arrogance. The confidence of a healthy young man who has never been hurt.

George had not been hurt either. Sometimes he thought – that's the trouble! Children pinch themselves, don't they, to make sure they're not dreaming? Not that he wanted to suffer; to starve, go to war, or to prison. But it did seem to him that his life was under a peculiar blight; that the important things happened while his back was turned, while he was eating, or sleeping, or quietly picking his nose and thinking his own, private thoughts. The day his father's ship went down, sunk by a German submarine in the North Sea the first, bitter winter of war, he had been playing with a pet rabbit in his grandmother's garden. When they dropped the bomb on Hiroshima, he was in bed with measles. His tongue was coated; his grandmother brought him bread and golden syrup and he cried because it tasted so horrible, mixed with the fur on his tongue. His grandmother was crying too. She said, 'All those poor people.'

His father, and all those poor people – but when, some years later, the adolescent George set himself to think about the moment of their deaths, what came into his mind first and foremost was a tame rabbit he had loved more than his father, and the physical memory of an unpleasantly coated tongue. This apparent lack of true feeling shamed him deeply. He cultivated an air of melancholy pride and boasted to Sam, 'I'm afraid I'm a bit of an emotional eunuch.'

'Don't be bloody ridiculous.'

'But I *am* bloody ridiculous. My *life* is bloody ridiculous!'

He felt this increasingly. He longed to be purposeful, of some clear use in the world. But however fast he ran, chance always whisked away round the corner.

The war, for one thing. He and Sam, ten years old at the end of it, were of an age to think they had missed something. But by the time they left school to do their National Service in Kenya, even the Mau Mau troubles were over. Nothing left except what were called 'mopping-up operations', which sounded (Sam said) more domestic than military.

George bought a second-hand Leica in Nairobi. He took some photographs of a baby elephant that had fallen into a ditch and been rescued by his unit, and sold the world rights to *Paris Match* for three hundred pounds. After this astonishing commercial success he took his camera with him whenever his platoon was sent into the bush for some foolish manœuvre or other. One day he was angling for an artistic closeup of a ten-foot-high, pinky-grey ant-heap, when a whirling dark shape burst out of a patch of scrub and charged straight at the man next in line to him. George, who had left his gun in the truck, swivelled round with his camera. The dramatic picture he took might have provided striking evidence at his court martial if it had not been for a telegram waiting for him back at camp, and the sympathetic attitude of his battalion commander to the news contained in it.

The telegram informed him that his mother was dead. She had been dying all the time George was in Kenya, playing at soldiers and taking photographs of baby elephants and ant-heaps and lance-corporals being torn apart by crazy buffaloes, and George had not known it. Discharged from the Army two months early, on compassionate grounds, he flew home and asked his grandmother why no one had told him. She said, 'We thought there was no point in your being unhappy, so far away.'

George thought he detected reproach in her voice. Perhaps she felt he should have known in some extra-sensory way that his mother was dying. His grandmother believed in psychic power. She had powers herself, of a sort: as a girl, she had been a water-diviner, she always knew when snow was coming, and once, standing on a cliff by the sea at Hunstanton in Norfolk, George had seen her tremble and turn pale. The ground had shifted beneath her, she said, and when they got back to the cottage she had rented for his summer holiday and turned on the radio, they heard there had been an earthquake in Turkey.

She was unusually sensitive to barometric pressure perhaps. There is a scientific explanation for everything. But remembering – in a soaring flash of absolute clarity – how miraculous the incident had seemed to him at the time, made George feel earthbound and guilty now; a lumbering, insensitive clod. What right had he to be angry with his grandmother? She had only done her innocent and loving best as she had always done; bringing him up while his mother worked, cooking and cleaning and playing with him like another child. In a second memory-flash George suddenly saw her flushed, pretty face many years younger, and heard her voice singing, 'If all the world were paper, and all the sea were ink . . .' Her face was old now, a used crumpled envelope, but a child still looked out from her eyes.

She said, 'I do hope I did right. But it would have made you so unhappy to see her as she was at the end. And there was nothing you could have done, was there?'

George saw the apprehensive, sixty-five year old child in his grandmother's eyes and couldn't tell her he felt cheated by the way yet another thing had happened behind his back; that he had loved his mother and would have liked to say goodbye to her. Instead, he kissed his grandmother, whom he loved too, and said of course she had done the right thing and went up to Oxford, on a government grant, to read modern languages.

Halfway through his first term, Sam Catto joined him. Sam was married by then to a girl he had met in Nairobi; an intelligent and beautiful girl called Claire, whose successful financier father had not cared for the idea of his expensively educated daughter marrying a grammar school boy with no money, but had made the best of it. He had said, Sam reported, 'I daresay a few years at the 'Varsity will polish Sam up a bit.'

He bought Claire a house in Holywell so that she could start married life comfortably and give little dinner-parties, which would be useful for Sam who had nothing behind him and couldn't begin too soon to meet the right people. 'There must be some of those, even in Oxford,' Claire's rich father said.

Claire didn't give dinner-parties. She and Sam lived in the biggest room in the house and let out the others to fellow students of whom George was one. They were all hugger-mugger and happy together: Sam-and-Claire, and George, and an Anglo-Indian girl with a lovely skin and pop eyes, and a handsome young Turk called Omer Kemal, who was reading Greats, and a rather weird young man from a private progressive school who smoked pot (which was an uncommon habit, then) and a pleasant, fat girl who came from the Midlands and intended to go into politics. This girl, Jane Derby, fell deeply and hopelessly in love with George, but he never knew this. He had no idea he was attractive to women.

Sam read medicine. He played rugger and put on weight and changed his accent to camouflage his lower-middle-class origins and impress his father-in-law. Taking as his model a bluff, old-fashioned medical tutor, he used quaint phrases like 'doncha know', and 'shouldn't wonder'. He was self-conscious at first, sometimes winking when he caught George's eye to show he knew it was only a joke, this absurd game of social mobility, but quite soon it became second nature and he could say 'old boy', or 'the wireless', without twitching an eyelid.

Watching Sam grow into his part of embryo surgeon, learning his lines, industriously fleshing the contours, George felt himself become sketchier daily; little more than a faint outline on the page. He grew a beard to make himself visible, joined the Labour Club and an experimental theatre group, and developed a trick of crinkling up his eyes when he smiled. But he still felt oddly insubstantial; a negative wraith in a world of positive people. Their certainties might be sometimes naïve, but his own lack of direction dismayed him.

Not that it mattered. How could it matter where he went, what he did? To take too much account of one's own life was ludicrous and George had a strong sense of the ludicrous.

He would never otherwise (so some of his friends said) have married his dreadful wife, Leila, and there was a small grain of truth in this. There was a ludicrous quality about their first meeting that made, you might say, a George-story (when he met his friends something absurd had often just happened to him) and although these stories were not always quite true, being a shy man's form of defence, perhaps, by the time he was thirty-six (the age when he married) he had invented a *style* for himself which sometimes affected his actions, although he preferred to think it explained them.

Like the story he told about the man in Rome . . .

When he was asked why he had gone into the travel business (it was mostly strange women who asked him this, idly inquisitive wives at suburban parties) he sometimes said one thing, sometimes another. If the tone of the questioner's voice suggested she thought it a quaint occupation (*her* man being a doctor, or a lawyer, or a producer in the BBC) he might say, 'Well, why not?' Or, 'Given a name like George Hare it was a logical development, don't you think? Hare's Travel – Swift and Sure!' But occasionally, when he was in the mood, or caught up in an intense eyeball-to-eyeball confrontation towards the end of a drunken evening, he would say, 'Well, you see, love, I met this man in Rome.'

George was twenty-one then; a tall, skinny young man, all knees and elbows, with a fair, curly beard. He had gentle manners, of a punctilious, rather old-fashioned kind, and a cheerful, hopeful smile. A cynic by persuasion, he was an optimist by nature: although he had accepted, intellectually, that life was a series of terrible jokes, he still couldn't help believing, secretly, that things would somehow turn out for the best. For him, anyway.

He had been reading French and Italian for three terms at Oxford and had found a job for the summer vacation with a travel agency. He was a courier, leading cultural tours round Italy. Vicenza, Venice, Florence, Rome.

The customers on these tours were mostly English ladies past their youth; schoolteachers or intelligent widows, uniformly equipped with pre-war guide books and flat shoes for museums, crumpled nylon macks against the chance of rain, and various ingenious devices, such as cloth pouches fastened round their waists, to keep their money safe. There were usually a few middle-aged couples, but rarely any single men. In fact, the only one George encountered that summer was the man he claimed to have met in Rome.

This man was in his forties – ancient, to George's eyes then – plump and pink-faced, with receding hair and a small, neat moustache. He had the professionally jaunty air of a retired military man, but according to George's records, he was a solicitor called William Barnet, with a practice in Slough. Although he had, actually, been with the tour since the beginning, he had been so little trouble that George had barely spoken to him. Other people lost their tickets, their raincoats, even (incredibly to George) their false teeth; they needed doctors, dentists, chiropodists, stamps and medicines, special food and lavatories at inconvenient moments, advice on where to buy souvenirs and on what they could take home free of duty through Customs, but William Barnet asked for nothing. He seemed contented enough, intelligent – at least he listened to the intelligent things George told his party about the art and architecture of Italy – and quite undemanding. George, who enjoyed being a good shepherd to his elderly flock, was not especially grateful for this.

The tour took ten days. They reached Rome on the seventh day and that evening was free – a kind of late half-term holiday. They arrived at the hotel at eight o'clock, dined at eight-thirty; most went to bed early.

George went walking. Not looking for girls, not looking for anything, except perhaps his own youthful self. For seven days he had kept pace with old people, anticipating their needs, the moment when backs would begin to tire, feet to swell, and it took him a little while to feel a young man again; to stretch his legs to full stride, open his lungs to the air.

Rome had delighted him ever since his first visit; from the moment he had seen for himself how tiny the Forum was. When they had acted *Julius Caesar* at school it had seemed so ridiculous, the way Cato and all the conspirators kept bumping into each other whenever they went out of doors, but when George stood on the site it made sense at once: the centre of the vast Roman Empire had been only the size of a village! He loved Rome for this discovery. He also loved it for its bustle and jostle and general urbanity, as much as for its blue skies and fountains and ponderous history. Surely there was no other city in the world where people smiled so much, or where all the girls looked like princesses? He knew most of them were probably poor, and had scrimped to buy just one expensive outfit each season, because it was so important to present a *bella figura*, but this vanity, which would have struck him as shallow in London or Paris, seemed quite proper in Rome: its citizens dressed beautifully to honour their beautiful city.

And it was easily the best European city to go walking in. Even now the traffic presented no problem since it was stationary so much of the time. All the same, George preferred the streets of the old town where there were no cars at all, and this evening he walked there, pleasurably, without purpose, turning at the end of each narrow street whichever way took his fancy, stopping occasionally to stare into shop windows and secretive courtyards and intimate restaurants.

He lingered outside one of these; a small pavement café with a striped awning. He was reading the menu when a voice spoke from behind a frieze of greenery. 'Care for a drink, would you?'

George saw William Barnet, grinning at him between two potted plants. His cheeks, normally rosy, had darkened to purple, and his eyes had red threads of blood in the corners.

George said, 'I didn't see you at dinner.'

Barnet shook his head. 'Had enough of all those fussy old biddies. Daresay you have too. Young chap like you, what a job, eh?'

'I enjoy it,' George said.

He joined him behind the plants. Once he had sat down Barnet fell silent. He poured wine for George, refilled his own glass, and then stared morosely in front of him, until his silence began to seem like a threat, and George felt that if he broke it, scraped his chair, cleared his throat, or made some amiable, inane remark, something fearful might happen; some terrifying eruption of rage or misery. He sat very still, gazing at his drink into which some small insect had fallen and was making surprisingly deep ripples with its cottony legs in an effort to keep floating. George dipped his forefinger into the wine and lifted the creature out. It seemed dead now, but might recover, he thought, when it had dried out a bit.

Barnet said, 'Hmm, hmm.' George looked up. 'What are you holding your finger like that for?'

George showed him. 'I can't just wipe the thing off, I might damage it, mightn't I? If it's still living, I mean.'

Barnet laughed incredulously. George blushed. He watched the thread-like corpse on his finger. He thought its back legs stirred slightly. Barnet said, 'If you put a leaf underneath, you won't hurt it.' He pulled a leaf off the plant in the tub by his chair and pushed it across the table. George eased the insect on to the leaf and tried to smile at the solicitor, feeling miserably embarrassed because he had blushed – he could still feel the giveaway heat in his cheeks.

Barnet regarded George with drunken affection. His moroseness seemed gone. He said, 'How old are you?'

'Twenty-one.'

'My boy's twenty today. That's what I'm drinking to. My only son's birthday. If you'd care to keep me company, I'd be obliged. I've another bottle on ice.'

George drained his glass obediently and Barnet refilled it. The wine was fizzy and sweet and left a metallic aftertaste on the tongue.

Barnet said, 'Not that he knows I'm his father, mind you. But I've watched him grow up. Always remembered his birthdays, taken him out to lunch in the holidays, that sort of thing. How'd you feel?'

16

'I'm not sure I know what you mean.'

Barnet scratched the side of his nose hard enough to raise a weal, examined his nail (to see if there was blood on it?) then belched loudly. George watched him, amazed: this middle-aged solicitor had seemed, up to now, such a fastidious man. Barnet said, in a tetchy voice, 'Well, it's not difficult. His mother's the wife of an old chum of mine who thinks *he*'s the father. That's it, in a nutshell.'

George didn't want to hear anymore but couldn't see how this could be managed. Barnet's inflamed eyes suggested he would take offence if George were to point out he might well be sorry he'd told him this story tomorrow. To do *that*, anyway, George would have to make it apparent he thought him drunk now – an impertinence that an elderly man would rightly resent, coming from a boy half his age. And George couldn't just get up and leave. That would be cruelly snubbing and his grandmother had brought him up to avoid hurting people. Besides, he was *responsible* for Barnet. If he were left to finish another bottle alone, he might be incapable of getting safely back to his hotel and his bed. Or worse, he might turn belligerent! George suddenly saw him, yelling at waiters, the police being summoned, Barnet spending a night in a Roman jail, and felt a chill run through his veins like iced water. *His blood running cold*, he thought, intellectually appraising the truth of this cliché. At the same time he realized that he had no choice but to sit it out, endure whatever hideous embarrassment was coming. It was a classic situation, he sometimes said, when telling this story, a classic plot for a nightmare. You are forced to stand helplessly by, unable to speak or act, while absurd events roll uncontrollably on . . .

The absurdity in this case (George always admitted it) was largely a question of age. He was young enough to feel faint disgust at the thought of anyone over about thirty-five having any real sexual involvements. By that age people should have given up sex (*passion*, certainly) and be calmly occupied with bringing up their children and perhaps contemplating their latter end. They shouldn't be getting drunk in foreign restaurants and tumbling skeletons out of cupboards in front of total strangers. Especially not men like William Barnet who would have regrets later. He was a buttoned-up, poker-backed Englishman; not the *type* . . .

Nor was he the type, it slowly appeared (slowly in George's version, anyway; a lot of the narrative being taken up with his own reactions at the time) to seduce his chum's wife light-heartedly, which made the whole thing more painful to listen to. He had taken the woman out to dinner (according to George, he called her 'the lady in the case') while her husband, a barrister, was away at Assizes. This was something he had often done; nothing new. But when they returned to her house for coffee and brandy, she sent the maid to bed (this was a middle-class house, in the 'thirties) and asked him to give her a baby. As a kindness. She and her husband longed for children but after seven years of marriage nothing had happened. They had seen doctors, taken tests, and finally been told the husband was sterile, but he refused to believe it. She said to Barnet, 'You must never tell him I've told you. He would never forgive me.'

Barnet had obliged her. (That was the word he used, George said. Obliged. 'I obliged the lady. Not just the one night, you know, but several nights running. No point in spoiling the ship for a ha'p'orth of tar. We sent the maid off to her sister in Ealing and did the job properly.')

The child was born nine months later. Barnet remained the family friend, visiting the house regularly, celebrating anniversaries (their wedding day, the child's birthdays), watching his son grow up. The boy began to look a little like him, he thought; or a little like he had looked when he was young. Barnet grew a moustache and, for safety's sake, destroyed all his old photographs. The wife never gave any indication by word or by look that their relationship had ever been other than it was now, and the husband never suspected. Or never appeared to suspect. Sometimes he would say to his friend, 'Isn't he like me, Bill? Don't you think he looks like me? Round the mouth, especially?'

George listened in sweating silence, hunched glumly under the brightly bleak café lights, drinking glass after glass of the sticky, metallic wine, and dreading the moment when he would have to say something. When it came, when Barnet said, 'Well, there you have it,' all George could manage was a foolish mumble about it being a terrible thing, really *terrible*, and being so sorry . . .

Barnet frowned at the bottle, held it up to the light, poured out the last dregs. 'Oh, you get used to it. Get used to anything. It's not as if I don't see the boy, and he seems to like me. Rather more than he likes his father, strictly between you and me! And the situation's not without pleasures, you know, though they're not necessarily ones a decent man would care to admit to unless he was tight as a tick. Power and so forth. I mean, I look at this old chum who's more successful in his branch of the law than I am in mine and grown a bit smug with it, and I think, *I've only to open my mouth!* Not that I shall, of course. What would the point be?'

He grinned affably at George; then, almost at once, his red-flecked eyes widened in unaffected, comical dismay. 'Though I've opened my mouth to you, haven't I? It's the first time, you know. I've never told a living soul until now. Until this blessed night!'

He seemed caught up in the wonder of this for a minute, staring at nothing while he emptied his glass and mopped his small, stiff moustache with a white linen handkerchief. He moistened his lips with his tongue and looked shyly at George. 'It's being on holiday, I suppose. Away from it all. You can say things to strangers.'

To the young George – young and slightly drunk – this simple statement appeared as a profoundly important truth. Or so he claimed later. Whether he really determined on his future career as a result of it, hardly matters. More irrevocable decisions are made in moments of drunken sentimentality than thoughtful people care to acknowledge. And the episode – as he told it, anyway – did express something; gathered up, made explicit, and somehow *respectable* what he would have been too shy to put forward as a sense of vocation. Though he did feel it. Had felt, all that summer, that he was not merely leading elderly ladies round souvenir shops, but acting as midwife to more spiritual adventures. In everyday life most people were drudges, cogs in machines; it was only on holiday that they had time to breathe, to explore wider horizons, freedom to find their real selves.

He had not found himself at Oxford. It had seemed like his grandmother's song to him; a world of paper and a sea of ink. When he was offered a permanent job at the end of the summer, he decided to take it. He wanted, he told himself, to do something useful, do good, if only in a small way. And a year later, when he opened his own bureau, he was somewhat less humble. Dentists repair teeth; doctors, bodies. Travel agents may, on occasion, repair lives.

He had no money. His grandmother, who would have given him the skin off her back, had he asked for it, was happy to sell her small, terraced house and lend him the proceeds. She had absolute faith in George because he was a man. She believed men understood what she thought of as 'business'. George bought a short lease on a shop in the High Street with a flat above it that had a nice, airy room for her, with a window-box so she should not miss her garden too much, and a narrow, dark room for him. This was a pleasant county town within reach of London, but separated from it by the Green Belt, inhabited by retired people, commuters to the City, and some poorer folk who worked locally, charring and gardening for rich families, or making white-wood furniture or electrical equipment at a couple of factories down by the station, carefully sited to spoil no one's view.

George determined that his agency should provide spiritual nourishment for all kinds and conditions of people. Most were slaves, in his view; he hoped to free them, if only for two weeks a year. He did not understand 'business'. His only qualification was a burning desire to show his fellow men the riches of the earth.

It was (luckily for him, perhaps) the beginning of the package deal boom.

He had hoped to make people happy, but he had not expected to become rich. That was something that happened while he was looking the other way. His agency was small and he kept it small to begin with; under his eye. For several years he opened no other branches, did not advertise, employed only one bright young man from the same grammar school he and Sam had attended, who took charge when he travelled, two girl typists and a spry, elderly lady who had been a headmistress and who did the accounts. Her name was Elspeth Tree, she had dyed, red hair, and was a mathematical genius, though that was not why George had engaged her. She shared his grandmother's interest in spiritualism; they had met at a séance, his grandmother had asked her to tea and told George her new friend was bored in retirement, that she had taught maths in school, understood book-keeping, and would be glad to help out in the office. George had taken her on to keep his grandmother happy.

If the world beat a path to his door it was because he had, in his missionary innocence, something to offer it. He knew that what people said they wanted was rarely what they did want in their hearts. They might ask for a seaside hotel in Spain with private bath and ham and chips three times a day, but what they secretly longed for, what they *needed*, was romance and excitement, beauty and truth. Some revelation of joy.

He became, behind the counter of his agency, something of a tyrant. He had no idea what was good for himself, could not take himself seriously enough to try and find out, but he knew what was good for his customers. He sent sedentary people on walking tours in the Pyrenees, factory workers who had never been taught ancient history to Ephesus and Mycenae, nervous couples who had never dared to travel further than Brighton because of the dangers of foreign food and water over the Atlas mountains and down to the Sahara in hired Land Rovers.

It should have been a recipe for disaster. But it seemed George had an instinct, a flair. 'George can read people's *over-souls*,' his grandmother said when Sam and Claire Catto came to visit one Sunday, bringing their small daughter with them.

Sam raised his eyebrows. 'What's that? Some kind of spiritual galosh?'

'What's a galosh?' his daughter asked. Her name was Sally and she was six years old.

'A kind of rubber boot to put on over your shoes when it's wet,' Elspeth said. She often came to the flat at weekends, ostensibly to help George's grandmother, or do a little extra work in the office, but really, George guessed, because she was lonely. He was used to her and fond of her but occasionally, as now, he saw her afresh, as a stranger might see her, and realized what a bizarre figure she cut: a big, mannish old woman with a floury, moon face and metallic red hair flicked up in stiff wisps like a great, rusty flower.

Sally said, 'Uncle George goes in the car when it's wet.'

Sam roared with laughter and Elspeth turned sharply towards him.

'Laugh away. George has a Gift. Mock as you bloody well like.'

'I wasn't mocking,' Sam said. But amusement still lurked in his eyes. He affected to think George's occupation a bit of a joke. A friend of his, plying his trade in the High Street! Introducing George at the parties he and Claire gave in the London house Claire's father had bought them when Sam got his first hospital job, he sometimes called him a 'travel tycoon'. George didn't mind this defensive extravagance. Although he didn't share it, he understood Sam's social uneasiness, having grown up with it. Meeting Claire's father for the first time in Nairobi, he had heard Sam say loudly, unasked, 'My father works on the railways.' Squaring up, as if for a fist fight.

He said, 'It's luck, really. Guess-work. I look at people when they come in and try and think what I'd like to do if I were them. Put myself in their place.'

'*Nice* George!' Claire smiled at him, through a blonde curtain of hair. Her lovely, sleepy-cat smile.

'I'm not nice,' he said irritably. 'I told you. I just guess!'

'Bloody profitably, I can tell you,' Elspeth said. 'If he goes on like this he'll be rich as sodding Croesus time he's finished.'

Leila (of course!) couldn't bear her. When George came home from the hospital after watching Elspeth die (fighting the oxygen mask they tried to put over her face, cursing and blinding to the last) Leila said, 'Your grandmother was such a refined little woman. I can't understand what she saw in that creature.'

'Can't you?' George asked this wonderingly. They had been married a year and he had not yet plumbed the depths of his wife's stupidity.

What his grandmother had seen in Elspeth was a comforting, masculine presence. Men shouted and swore and smoked, dropping ash on the carpets. George had never done any of these things; Elspeth did them all. She smoked long, thin black cigars constantly, drank malt whisky in extraordinary quantity, and swore like a trooper if she was interrupted when she was reading the *Financial Times*. She was the perfect complement for George's grandmother, who was gentle and loving and silly. They made (in effect, only) a sweet old Lesbian couple, and when George bought a Queen Anne house he had long admired at the top of the High Street, renovated it and divided it in two, Elspeth sold her cold, riverside bungalow and moved into one half of it with his grandmother, who had confessed to being lonely, sometimes, when George was abroad.

For the first time in his life (at nearly thirty) George had a separate, bachelor establishment. It felt strange at first. His grandmother had always ordered their domestic life, cooking large, regular, suety meals he was not always ready for, worrying over his excellent health and removing his clothes to wash before they were dirty. Surrounding him, in general, with a soft, cushiony concern that had often stifled him, but he found he missed now. He got up in the morning, washed and shaved (he had abandoned his beard by this time) cooked his own breakfast, turned on the radio . . .

His grandmother could never bear to hear the news at breakfast. She would say, 'Leave it till later in the day, dear. We'll have more strength for it then.'

George missed hearing her say these ridiculous things. Sometimes he felt almost resentful of Elspeth. Though not so much, perhaps, because she had taken over his grandmother (he could see her any time he wanted, after all) but because she seemed to be taking him over, too. She persuaded him to expand his agency. He explained that he didn't want to, that he liked being a small concern, a lone pedlar of dreams in one market place, but he was too afraid of sounding sentimental to press this, and she was too absorbed in her own visions to listen. She was in love, this absurd, coarse, clever old woman, with the choreography of figures: while she spoke to George about adventure capital and limited companies and merchant banks, he could see by the look in her eyes that she was mesmerized by some marvellous ballet taking place in her head.

He gave in. He didn't care enough not to. What did it matter, after all? Let money make money – it seemed that after a certain stage it was self-propagating, like a ginger-beer plant. He developed his original building, taking in the flat above it to make larger offices, and appointed two directors; the bright grammar school boy and Jane Derby, the nice, plain, fat girl who had been at Oxford with him. Her political ambitions had come to nothing; she had become an economist at the Board of Trade and had married unhappily. George met her, one spring evening in Athens, sitting alone at a café in Syntagma Square and weeping because her husband had left her.

George bought her dinner and took her on a trip he had planned round Southern Greece. They enjoyed each other's company, in bed and out, and George felt, being old-fashioned in some ways, that he should ask her to marry him, but she had had enough of marriage, she said. Enough, too, of the Board of Trade. Climbing up to the ruined citadel above the hill town of Monemvasia, through wild flowers and thistles and silky, blonde grasses, she turned to George, flushed and breathless, and announced her intention to resign from the Civil Service in the rapt tones of someone who has just been granted miraculous guidance.

George was grateful to her for turning him down, although something about the way she had done it – a slight, watchful hesitation for perhaps half a minute – suggested that if he were to ask her again she might change her mind. He offered her a job instead and didn't regret it. She was sensible and reliable; imaginative enough to understand how he felt about what he was doing, and tough enough to stand between him and the grammar school boy, who thought George a bit of a nut case, though he called him eccentric. 'Eccentric fellow, old Hare. D'you know he won't advertise? No need, he says; word of mouth's all you want. Though he goes round himself with little cards he's had printed – leaves them in taxis and trains and in people's pockets in cloakrooms. Lucky he's not been arrested for suspicious behaviour.'

George knew he was laughed at and didn't care. Why should he? He knew himself to be comic; knew he was turning into a character. A man living alone had to do that: how else could he measure himself, know where he stood? Particularly by the time he was over thirty, and should have found out. And it was, too, a kind of politeness to others not to burden them with the sort of doubts that sometimes stopped him dead when he caught sight of himself, in an unexpected mirror or in a shop window, when he was striding along the street, and thought – *Good God, is that me?* All anyone would have seen when that happened was a tall, youngish man with a sweet, bony face and rather long, fair hair, limply blowing, suddenly changing direction for no obvious reason and darting erratically across the road in the thick of the traffic.

He wasn't unhappy. He enjoyed travelling; meeting old friends and new people; was excited by the promise of a packed suitcase, an air or train ticket. His favourite countries were Greece and Turkey, and since their tourist industries were still comparatively under-developed this preference tied in happily with commercial advantage. He was interested in the intermittent political upheavals in that part of the world, but only as an observer. He was shocked when the junta came to power in Greece, but could see no good reason for boycotting the new regime by not sending tours there although Jane argued, at first, that they should. What was the point? Greece had not been such a civilized regime before the colonels took over. If Hare's Travel withdrew, fastidiously, the hem of its prosperous garment, the only effect would be to impoverish the lives of already poor people: waiters, taxi-drivers, the families who ran small taverns. And this apart, it was surely as much of an impertinence to make high moral gestures of this kind as it would be to bustle in and try to reorganize a friend's house one was visiting?

When he was at home, he lived in a safe shell of small habits, small pleasures. He saw Claire and Sam at least once a week. He dined with his grandmother and Elspeth on Thursday evenings and drove them into the country for lunch on Sundays. He liked clothes and bought a great many although he always looked vaguely shabby: once he'd worn a new suit for an hour, it looked as if he had rolled in a ditch in it. He looked after his house single-handed, doing his own cleaning and shopping and cooking, partly because he was mildly embarrassed by the idea of employing a servant, of using his money to buy this old-fashioned kind of class privilege, but mainly because he enjoyed doing these things for himself.

He enjoyed shopping especially, pushing his wire trolley round the bright, loaded shelves of the new supermarket, and watching the other shoppers: the busy, young mothers impatiently filling their baskets with one eye on the baby, and more cautious, elderly women and retired couples, carefully checking purchases against prepared lists, or putting on spectacles (fumbling, with gloved hands) to examine prices. Contriving, perhaps, to manage a winter week in Majorca?

These older people attracted George's particular attention. They moved slowly and he had time to observe them. And because he was close to his grandmother, closer to old age, because of his upbringing, than most men of his generation, he felt he knew how their minds worked, and this made him tender towards them. That upright pair now – the short perky woman with a pudgy, intelligent face, and her dignified, heavy-nosed husband – they would be bored stiff in Majorca! They would do better to try Venice, in spring. If money was tight, he knew a small pension near the Frari, though unless they were deaf, they would need ear plugs and sleeping pills. The great bell boomed out all night, on the hour.

He carried cards with him – the cards his co-director thought so amusing – and sometimes, when he saw what seemed a possible customer, he would slip a card into their trolley and feel a glow afterwards, as if he had surreptitiously given them a present. As perhaps he had, he once said to Leila, before he knew it was a mistake to confess his childish follies to her. She sighed and laughed in the odd way she had (apparently from the roof of her mouth) and said, 'George, you are so absurd! Really!'

Chapter 2

George's thirty-sixth birthday was a fine, April Friday with a gentle breeze blowing. He did his weekend shopping as usual, in the afternoon between three-thirty and four, transferred it from the wire trolley into two thick paper carrier-bags supplied by the supermarket, and left by the entrance which led to the car park.

Conscientiously leaving the area near to the store for older or more encumbered customers, he had left his car at the far end of the park, between a new Ford Estate and an elderly Bentley. The Bentley had been moved and a Volkswagen parked in its place, unnecessarily close to his yellow Saab. Only mildly irritated (he saw his own, rather pedantic thoughtfulness as a purely private indulgence and did not expect it from others) he squeezed between the two cars and managed, with difficulty, to open the door of the Saab and fold his long body into the driving seat.

Backing out carefully, he felt his front offside wheel bump against something. *Over* something. He got out, feeling sick, and saw the hind legs of a cat sticking out. It was clear of the wheel and he pulled it out easily, realizing with relief, that he had not killed it. It was quite stiff already, and the open, amber eyes were dusty.

Not his fault, then. Not that it mattered – not to the cat! But he was responsible now. Whoever had pushed it out of sight under his car, he couldn't leave it there now, rigid with death, in full view on the tarmac.

The supermarket was only recently finished. Beyond the edge of the car park was a patch of uncleared, scrubby land; a dump for builder's rubble, old baths, broken bricks, cracked lavatory pans. Perhaps the cat had been hit on the road and crawled there to die?

George emptied out one of his paper carriers, spilling the groceries on to the back seat of the Saab. He put the dead cat into the bag, left it beside the car, and went back into the store.

The manager was serving on the liquor counter. George knew him – not as a friend, but in some ways he knew more about him than he would ever know about a man he considered a friend. He had arranged his annual holiday for five years now; sent him to Cyprus, to Sardinia, to Yugoslavia and twice to Tunisia. He knew how much he could afford to spend, that he was sexually excited by veiled Arab women ('It gets the old pecker up, just thinking of what's there underneath, don't you find that, Mr Hare?') and the names and ages and tastes of his wife and two daughters. His older girl was at a teacher training college (the second Tunisian holiday, embarked on to satisfy her father's concupiscence, had been timed to give her a break before her final examinations at school) and the other was still young enough to qualify for a cheaper fare.

The manager was serving a middle-aged lady in a brown coat with two bottles of Highland Malt. While George waited patiently, he observed the bent, bald head, tonsured like a monk's, and imagined it reddened and freckled by the North-African sun. Perhaps he covered it, wore a straw hat or a white, folded handkerchief as he strolled in the casbah, lagging behind his family to eye the dark, shrouded women. His pecker lifting between his shrivelled thighs. Had he made love to his wife more often since then, George wondered – and felt self-conscious as the man turned to him at exactly that moment, smiling with brisk servility. 'Now, Mr Hare. I'm sorry to have kept you.'

George explained about the cat. 'If you've got a spade, I'll bury it.'

The manager's smile grew indulgent. 'Well, that's nice of you, Mr Hare. I think there's a builder's shovel still out the back in a barrow, but I wouldn't take the trouble if I was you. Tell you straight.' He laughed complacently.

'It's no trouble,' George said. 'Really.'

The shovel was heavy and blunt – had been used for mixing concrete. And although the ground was soft on the surface, it was solid clay a spade's depth down. George had time to reflect on the folly of acting on impulse. What was the point of burying the creature anyway? Who was he sparing, and for what purpose? Anyone could see worse sights than a dusty, dead cat, almost any time they turned on the telly.

Still, he had put his hand to the plough and had dug deep enough. He put the spade down and returned for the cat. But the carrier-bag that contained it had gone.

Or was not where he'd left it. The Volkswagen parked so inconveniently close to his Saab had its bonnet up and a woman was stowing her shopping away. His dead cat, too – picked up by mistake, presumably. She had several, similar carriers with the store's name printed on them.

He said, 'Excuse me,' and the woman turned with an intake of breath. A delicate, rather sallow face with remarkably large, dark-rimmed, tragic eyes. George thought – like some small, nocturnal animal. He said, 'I'm terribly sorry but I'm afraid you've picked up my bag.'

The eyes snapped. They were a beautiful, rich, smoky-blue; the dark rims, painted on, made them seem like weapons of war. She said, 'And *I'm* afraid you're quite wrong!'

George was amused by her insulted air. He said, 'Are you so sure? I think it's that one. Why not look?'

She tightened her mouth. Her face was older than her eyes; pinched with outrage, she looked at least forty. She dropped the bag she was holding and wrenched the sides open. She stared into it.

George said, 'You see? Was I really mistaken?' Laughter made his voice tremble.

She looked up, quite defenceless. Her embattled eyes stared at George; then suddenly seemed to lose focus. He said, 'Steady on,' but moved towards her too late. She crumpled untidily, falling backwards against the Volkswagen, then to the ground.

She lay still, on her side, one arm trapped beneath her, the other hitched up in some way on the car's bumper. George bent over her, feeling foolish. Her eyes were closed and she was making an odd, whistling sound through her nose. He released the sleeve of her blue, woollen dress that was caught up on the bumper and straightened her legs and arms to make her more comfortable. He thought he shouldn't move her too much. Perhaps she had hit her head when she fell. It was an old wives' tale that people did not hurt themselves when they fainted. Why had she fainted, anyway? It seemed an exaggerated reaction. Perhaps she had a heart condition?

Several people were standing round now. A woman said, 'I saw what happened. She just keeled straight over, didn't she? Out like a light. You ought to get a doctor to her if she doesn't come round in a minute.'

The manager was still serving on the liquor counter. There was a queue waiting. George pushed to the front of it and said, 'May I use your telephone to call an ambulance, please?'

The manager lifted the flap of the counter and waved

George through to the office beyond. He was looking astonished. George said, 'Oh, no. Not for the *cat*!'

He dialled the Emergency Services and got a crossed line. A woman said, 'You'll see to the bridge rolls then, and I'll do the cake. Fruit, I thought. It keeps better. If that'll suit Edna. I mean, I don't suppose it matters to Jack one way or the other.'

George depressed the receiver, waited, then dialled again. The same voice continued, 'Well, if you think she'd rather a Victoria sponge, then it's all one to me. Though if it turns hot the cream might go off and I must say I think fruit's nicer myself. Especially for a mixed do. But it's up to Edna, of course. She's the one. Just get her to make up her mind.'

Another female voice said, 'Well, you know Edna!'

Both women laughed, at some length.

George said, 'I'm sorry to interrupt you but I'm trying to ring for an ambulance. Someone's been hurt.'

There was a short silence. Then the first voice said, 'Excuse *me*, but we are conversing!'

'Yes,' George said. 'I'm sorry. But this is an emergency. Would you mind putting the telephone down?'

He did so himself. He counted to thirty. When he dialled again, they had gone; the number was ringing.

It rang and rang. He listened, biting the flesh at the side of his thumb nail. After a minute, he replaced the receiver and dialled the operator. There was a *click* and then nothing.

The manager said, from the doorway, 'We've had this all morning. They're doing something at the Exchange. I kept getting some bloke in Hull. *He* was trying to 'phone Liverpool. Took me three-quarters of an hour to get through to Head Office.'

George tried again. The silence outraged him. And his own helplessness. He said, 'Oh, bugger it all. This is bloody ridiculous.'

'Mechanization,' the manager said, with quiet satisfaction. 'It's always the same. Anything I can do, Mr Hare?'

'Just keep trying, please,' George said. 'There's a woman unconscious out there on the tarmac.'

Dying perhaps? A coronary? He left the store at a run. The April breeze had strengthened; blew his hair into his eyes. He thought – time I had a haircut. Then – what am I running for?

As he ran, tossing his hair back, he saw an ambulance turn out of the car park, blue light flashing.

A small crowd was dispersing. The woman who had spoken to him earlier, before he went to telephone, was waiting by the Volkswagen. She said, 'It's all right. A policeman came by and he called up an ambulance on his radio. I was coming to tell you.'

She beamed in a motherly way. She had a plump, friendly, open face. 'She'll be all right, not to worry! She came round just after you'd gone but they took her off just the same. It's best to make sure, you know.'

'Oh yes,' George said. 'Yes, of course.'

'Hospital's the best place when you've had a funny turn. After all, you can't always tell, can you?'

'No. I suppose not.'

She looked at him doubtfully. 'You didn't want to go in the ambulance with her? I mean, she wasn't a friend of yours, was she?'

George shook his head.

'That's what I thought. The policeman asked, was there anyone with her, and I told him no, she was all by herself. I knew you'd spoken to her but I assumed you'd just asked her to move her car so you could get out, and there didn't seem any point in going into all that.'

'No,' George said. 'Thank you.'

'*That*'s all right, then. I thought for a moment I'd made

a mistake. Jumped to conclusions. I'm a terror for that, so my family say. You ought to hear my children on the subject of their mother!'

She paused. George smiled, as it seemed he was expected to, and she laughed merrily in answer, shaking her head in comic dismay and pretending to wipe a tear from the corner of one eye.

'But as I say to them, I'm usually *right*! And what's the point in going the long way round when you can cut a few corners? I said to myself, that young man won't want to hang about, answering silly questions from policemen, he'll want to get off. And so you can, now. The policeman moved her car out of your way.'

George looked. The Volkswagen was neatly parked at the edge of the tarmac. Its boot was closed. The ground around it was clear.

He said, 'There was a carrier-bag . . .'

'Oh, he saw to everything. Put all her stuff away in the car and locked it up for her before she went off in the ambulance. So you don't have to worry.'

And he didn't have to, of course! Thoughtfulness, carried to extremes, could be a kind of narcissism. Any woman fool enough to faint at the sight of a dead cat deserved all she got. Except, perhaps, coming back to her car and finding the creature still there, neatly locked up in the boot with her shopping . . .

He could go to the police. They would have a skeleton key. 'Can you imagine it, though?' he said to Claire, telephoning to say he would be late for the dinner-party she and Sam had arranged for his birthday. 'Having to explain the whole thing step by awful step to Constable Plod at the station?'

'I don't believe it. I just don't *believe* it, George darling.'

Claire's voice shook with delight. He pictured her laughing; standing in the narrow hall of her pretty house, the telephone receiver nestling against her smooth cheek. Lovely, laughing Claire; grey-blonde hair swinging.

She said, 'Try not to be too late, though. Sally wants to stay up and she has her drama class early tomorrow.'

'I'll be there, tell her.'

'Tell her yourself. She's listening on the extension. Soon as she knew it was you, she bolted upstairs.'

Sally said, 'Shut up, mother.'

George thought – *Sally*! Fifteen years old; blonde like Claire, cool and sweet. An ice-maiden.

Her voice was low, slightly hoarse. 'Happy birthday, Uncle George. Do you feel ancient?'

'Old as the hills.'

'I think thirty-six is a marvellous age for a man,' Claire laughed. Sally said, 'Oh, go *away*, mother. It's my *turn*. Put the telephone down.'

Claire said, 'See you later, George darling.'

Sally waited for the click. Then said, 'What's this bloody cat-woman like?'

'I hardly had time to examine her. She had pretty eyes.'

'Bitch,' Sally said. 'She sounds fucking awful.'

George was silent. Sally said, in a pleased voice, 'Are you shocked, Uncle George?'

'Yes.'

'Fifteen year old girls shouldn't swear? Uncle George Prissy-boots.'

'It shows a lack of imagination.'

'Oh God. I wish I was *forty*. It's humiliating, being my age. Mustn't swear, mustn't be jealous. Promise me one thing. Don't get involved with her, will you?'

'Don't be daft, Sally-kins.'

'Sally *darling*.'

George hesistated. 'Sally, darling. Darling Sally. Nice women don't ask for endearments.'

Sally chuckled. George felt his bowels melting.

'I must go,' he said. 'If I'm not to be too late tonight.'

'If you're later than half-past eight I'll kill myself. I swear I will. Jump out of the window or cut my wrists in the bath.'

George thought of Sally in the bath. She was taller than her mother and had fuller breasts. He closed his eyes briefly. He said, in a dry voice, 'I'll bring a wreath, just in case,' and put the phone down.

Her name was Leila Charles. This was a small cottage hospital and she was the only casualty brought in that day who had been kept in. George advanced down the ward with a bunch of red tulips and she smiled when she saw him.

She looked much younger in bed than she had looked in the car park. Waif-like, with huge eyes. They had put her into a hospital gown laced up to the throat and tied her thick, reddish hair back with a ribbon.

She said, 'I feel such a fool . . .'

'Are you all right?' He put the flowers down on the bed and stood awkwardly.

'They're keeping me in overnight. Not because there's anything wrong, really, just a bump on the head, and no damage to show on the X-ray. I'm afraid, to tell you the truth, that they've written me off as a rather hysterical lady! But they've been wonderfully kind, all the same, and it's such a treat to be fussed over!'

'Well, it's best to make sure,' he said, echoing the woman in the car park. He repeated the rest of that conversation and was pleased to see her smile. He said, 'So if you'll trust me with your car keys, I'll go and remove the evidence from the boot. I'll return the keys to the hospital, or bring the car here, if you'd rather.'

'Oh, you are *kind*!' She laughed; she had a pretty laugh. 'Though there's no need, as it happens. In fact what they did was to put the – the *bag* into the ambulance. They didn't find out what was in it until we got to the hospital. It caused a lot of amusement. You can imagine!' Her smoky eyes darkened. 'When I was little, my brother once found a dead cat on the beach and chased me with it, to tease me. I suppose that was partly why ...' She stopped; smiled bravely, and shivered.

'I'm a clumsy idiot,' George said, feeling this deeply.

She shook her head. 'You could have hardly known you were dealing with such a sensitive soul! What I thought was that *you* thought I was pinching your shopping! That's what made me so spiky! This strange man looming up and accusing me! I'm always scared of being thought a shop-lifter. It's the sort of thing women my age go in for, you see. Just to go into those stores that have television cameras makes me feel shifty! Big Brother watching you!'

She shivered again; smiled appealingly. George felt protective. He said, 'Can I do something? Ring your family.'

She shook her head. 'I'm afraid my husband and I were divorced last year. I live alone now.'

'I'm sorry,' George said.

'It takes getting used to. I'm over the worst of it, but when something like this happens, it brings it home, rather. Having no one to turn to. There's my brother, of course, but he lives in Scotland and I'd have to be *dying*! We're not over-fond of each other.' She picked up the tulips and looked at him sadly. 'Thank you for these. I can't remember when someone last brought me flowers! Not that I like them in the house, really, I get such dreadful hay fever, but it's the thought, isn't it? I'm so grateful to you.' Her eyes moistened. 'I can't tell you how grateful ...'

George felt trapped. 'It's nothing. I mean, the flowers are

nothing. It was my fault you were hurt, after all. And I'm sorry about it.' He stopped. Those tragic eyes watched him. He said, 'Look – let me come and pick you up tomorrow. You may still feel a bit groggy.'

'I couldn't possibly let you do that. You've been too kind already. Don't feel responsible, because you're not. Really.'

She spoke crisply, as if she meant this. Damp-eyed still, but gallantly smiling. Her sorrows were none of his business. He was free to go; free as air.

'But I enjoy feeling responsible,' George said firmly.

When he left the hospital, he picked up Jane Derby, who had once been his mistress and was now simply an old friend and partner, and drove into London for Sam and Claire's dinner.

Jane wore a long dress of blue crêpe beneath which various tighter garments arranged her pleasant, plump flesh in firm rolls and hillocks. Claire was wearing white; Sally, a red dress of thin, Indian silk through which her nipples showed. She had piled her hair on top of her head and looked, not like a woman of thirty, but as a woman that age would have been delighted to look. She offered George her soft, unpainted mouth. He dodged it neatly, kissed her cheek with a loud, smacking sound, and said, 'Well, how's Sally?'

'Full of Eastern promise, as you see,' Sam said. 'Old as sin and young as the morning.'

Sam was expressing, George knew, only glowing pride and affection, but he was shocked, all the same. Claire saw him frown.

She said, 'It's a purely At-Home garment, that.'

'So I should bloody well hope,' Sam said. 'A walking incitement to rape.'

'Don't be disgusting, please Daddy,' Sally said. But she

had coloured a little; the faintest tinge on her close-textured, lily-pale skin.

George said boisterously, 'How's school, then?' and she rolled her eyes upwards.

'Need you ask? I mean, the only other time in your life you'd be forced to attend the same stinking place day after day would be if you'd broken the law and got sent to *prison*. You couldn't be more bored sewing mailbags, or whatever the poor sods do now! That's why most of us go onto drugs or get pregnant!'

'Sally is head of the school dramatic society and captain of Junior Netball,' Claire said. She laid slight, amused stress on the word *junior*. 'Not quite the anti-establishment figure she'd like you to think.'

'I make the best of things, you know that's all. I do think you're *rotten*,' Sally said in a high, furious voice. She glowered at her mother. The contrast between her childish anger and her fully formed body was striking. They all looked at her, they couldn't help it, and she knew why they were looking. Her blush deepened and her hands fluttered briefly in front of her breasts. Self-consciousness made her utterly beautiful.

George gazed like the others but despised himself for it. His shame bordered on rage. Oh, the prurient sexuality of middle-aged people! Sitting here, gawping at this lovely child. Warming their old bones at her fire, getting their slow juices flowing. Even her mother – gloating, like Juliet's nurse!

Claire met his eyes. She laughed lightly and said, 'Sally, love, go and light the candles and we'll come and have dinner.'

They dined by candlelight in the red and gold basement dining-room. George re-told the story about the dead cat for

Sam's benefit. Sam laughed a great deal. He said, 'Trust old George! Who else could it happen to?'

Sally went to bed and the room seemed dimmer without her. But they were easier in her absence; four old friends talking, and finishing the wine. If Sam and Claire talked mainly about her, that was perhaps natural: always doting, they seemed besotted this evening. In spite of fashionable complaining, Sally did well at school; was ambitious and clever. Weak at science, unfortunately: Sam had hoped she'd do medicine. Though he wouldn't persuade her, of course. 'Wouldn't work if I tried,' he said. 'She's stubborn, like me.'

Claire said quickly, 'She wants to do languages. French of course, and now Turkish! That's the latest craze at her school. A spin-off from the drug scene, I rather suspect. The London–Katmandu run. Though that's something we're really not worried about as far as Sally's concerned. She's too aware of the dangers.'

'Touch wood,' Sam said.

'Oh God, *yes*!' Claire clutched at the table-top; closed her eyes prayerfully. Opening them, she smiled at George. 'The thing is, some of her friends are going off camping in Turkey this summer, but they're mostly older than she is – most of her friends are, as a matter of fact – and we've told her she can't go. That hasn't made us very popular as you can imagine and we've more or less promised we'll arrange a trip for next year. But we'd rather she went to a family. Can you help, George? Do you think Omer would know someone?'

Omer Kemal had been with them at Oxford; had lived in Claire's house in Holywell. Sam and Claire had not seen him since then; George saw him whenever he went to Istanbul. He was going to Turkey next month. As Claire knew.

She said, 'He was such a nice little man. Bouncy as a cork. What's he like now?'

He was still bouncy. A little fatter each time George had seen him; energetic and merry. He had been an archaeologist, a politician (but only briefly: he was too Europeanized for the current political climate) and was a businessman now. He had started a scheme for Home Ownership backed by Unit Trusts that had been very successful – like George, he was a philanthropist who made money. He had married two years ago; a young wife.

But Claire was not really interested in Omer. George found he resented this faintly. He said, 'Just a Turkish business man. No useful daughter, I'm afraid. No children at all.'

Claire widened her eyes at his tone. 'I'm sorry. For *his* sake. We were so fond of him.'

George grinned at her and she laughed.

She said, 'He'd know someone, though, wouldn't he? Some Turkish girl who'd like to come here as an exchange? Sally could show her London. Teach her English.'

'Teach her a few other things I daresay, some that old Omer might not be quite so enthusiastic about.' Sam winked at George in the candlelight. 'Turkish girls are pretty protected. Lock up your daughters!'

George said, 'Is that such an unreasonable parental attitude?' and Sam and Claire laughed at him kindly.

Driving Jane Derby home, George said, 'I feel quite irrelevant suddenly. Do you ever feel irrelevant, Jane?'

A passing lamp showed her broad face smiling placidly. 'It's married couples with children. Their assumption that childless lives must be empty. Even if they don't think it, they feel it. It's a visceral thing – *they* won't leave this earth unsatisfied!'

'I think it's more of a moral issue as they see it. An assumption of virtue. They've performed their biological duty,

42

kept the race going, and so they're one up on people like you and me. Our only function is to fix their kids up with jobs, trips abroad. Not that I mind.'

Jane laughed. She sounded quite happy. Perhaps she was. She enjoyed her job, her pretty house by the river. She had a middle-aged lover, a married man who came when he could. Was she happy with him? George glanced sideways and wondered. He knew her so well and yet he knew nothing. How could you know anything, beyond question and answer? Would you want to? The thought of other people's independent existence was ultimately shocking. To be free of another imagination might prove too much for one's own – the mind would crackle and fuse like an overloaded electrical circuit. Safer to stay locked inside one's own lighted skull . . .

Jane said, 'You should get married, George. You've hung about on the fringe of other people's marriages far too long. It suits me, but not you. I watched you tonight! You envy Sam, don't you?'

She spoke calmly and as if she were much older than he was; a kind, privileged aunt, giving advice.

'I didn't think I did,' George said. 'Although I'm fond of Claire . . .'

'I didn't mean you envied him Claire.'

George cleared his throat and drove fast down a suddenly clear stretch of road. So much faster than usual that Jane put out a hand to the dashboard. When he finally slowed at a traffic light, she said in a nervous voice, 'I really don't know what I did mean.'

'You meant Sally.'

'Well,' she said, smiling defensively. 'Well. Yes, of course I did.'

'Why do you think I should envy Sam that packet of trouble?'

43

'I don't know. I don't know why I said that.' She frowned, but the reason, if there had been one, eluded her now. She said, 'Perhaps I was just trying to bring up the subject. Sally and you.'

'She's just a little tease. Little tart, little tease. Girls that age often are.'

The lights changed and he moved off, grinding the gear. 'Uncle George is fair game. It'll do her no harm to practise on me. She'll grow out of it.'

Jane said, 'I wasn't thinking of Sally. She can look after herself. Like her mother. I was thinking of you.'

He said nothing.

She sighed. 'George – don't be angry.'

'I'm not.'

'Well, then. You know what I mean. You're dotty about the child.'

'What's wrong with that?'

'Oh, it's none of my business. But it's bad for you, at your age – a silly hang-up over a schoolgirl.' She paused and added, quite angrily, 'I'm *fond* of you, George.'

'I know.' He groped for her plump hand, held it briefly against his cheek, then put it back in her lap. 'All right, then. What should I do, Jane?'

She said – promptly, as if she had thought about this – 'Keep away for a bit. Change your social habits. Meet some new people.'

'Easy as that?'

She chose to misunderstand him. 'Not where we live, I know. Everyone's too busy pruning their roses. I don't see you joining the golf club or taking pottery classes. But you're not tied. You could live in London for a while. Take a flat in Hampstead, say. Go to parties and meet some young women.'

George laughed rather louder and longer than the comic

simplicity of this remedy perhaps warranted. He said, 'I've been to parties in Hampstead. They're usually full of Jewish women in saris.'

'How peculiar,' Leila said, when he repeated this remark to her. Whenever she said 'how peculiar', or 'how absurd', she raised her eyebrows and her short upper lip. This response seemed to imply a distinct moral judgement, even if its nature was not always clear.

It flustered George, who had only meant to amuse. Did she think he was anti-Semitic? He said, appalled, 'Well, you know what I mean.'

'I'm very much afraid that I don't.' She laughed in her special, nasal, condescending way, suggesting that although she regretted this lack of comprehension herself, it could be considered, by thoughtful people, to be a subtle form of virtue.

He said, 'It was only a silly joke.'

'I'm sorry.' She shook her head, smiling ruefully. 'It's no good, George, I'm a lost cause, I'm very much afraid! I have *absolutely* no sense of humour!'

He found this unusual admission engaging. It made him re-think his own attitudes – always a healthy proceeding. What had he meant, after all? A form of cultural confusion that he found mildly risible? But that kind of flip, shorthand statement was hardly worth analysing. It was refreshing to have this brought home to him.

He found her refreshing in general, not only because she didn't laugh at his jokes and so showed him how unfunny they were. She seemed to him, in all things, amazingly, almost shockingly, truthful. Even her self-centredness looked to him like a certificate of honesty, as did another quality he had never been so close to before: a quality of desperation.

She had no pretences at all, didn't mind letting him see she was in despair at the way her life had turned out, that she saw no future for herself at all, and this moved him deeply. Reticence and pride could be admirable sometimes but they were more often mere affectations of a conventional kind: you were told one thing but expected to believe the unspoken opposite. When Leila spoke of her failed marriage she didn't say, 'Of course we were both at fault,' but, 'Roland was the most frightful brute. He treated me dreadfully.'

He drank. He knocked her about. She had a scar on her arm where he'd thrown a carving knife at her because she had not cleaned his shoes as he liked them. He had lovers (men as well as women) and told her about them in detail. But she was still sorry he'd left her. She said 'It sounds stupid in this day and age but I'm afraid I'm not suited for anything except marriage, really. No Women's Lib for yours truly! I like pottering about a house and looking after a man. I'm a natural handmaiden!'

She was working as a dentist's receptionist and hated it. You need stamina for that kind of uncreative job and she wasn't strong physically. There was nothing else she could do; no course of training that would accept her, at almost forty. No – there was nothing ahead except years of un-skilled labour, declining health and increasing loneliness. The advice columns urged widows and divorcées to get out and about but that was easier said than done. Single women were an embarrassment to their friends. The first months after Roland had left her she had been asked out, though usually to what were obviously second-class social occasions – family suppers, Sunday lunch-time drinks with miscel-laneous neighbours – but now even these invitations had stopped: she sat at home night after night and the telephone never rang. People were frightened of failure, perhaps –

as if losing a husband was a contagious disease! And of course married women did have cause to be nervous. The number of times men she had thought of simply as friends had brought her home after a party and expected her to have sex with them! Just a quick bash before they went back to their wives! As a favour to *her*! Sometimes they said, 'Come on old girl, you must be missing it!' But none of these disadvantages were the real reason for regretting Roland. She said, 'I'm afraid I still love him. Ridiculous, isn't it?'

The innocence of this declaration (innocent, because she didn't seem to see how vulnerable it made her) won George over completely. It also enlivened what might have been, otherwise, too dispiriting a picture even for him to contemplate. No one who is still able to love can be totally pitiable.

Not that she asked for pity. At least, not directly. Indignation was her response to the way life had treated her and she wielded it like a weapon as she rushed into battle. The first time George took her out to dinner, she sent her steak back because it was red in the centre. The waiter said, 'But you asked for medium, madam.'

'Medium doesn't mean freshly torn from a corpse, does it? And when it's properly cooked, I'd like it served on a clean, hot plate, if you please.' When the waiter had gone, she looked proudly at George. 'I'm afraid I've embarrassed you.'

'Of course not.'

'Being a woman alone, you learn to stand up for yourself. Restaurants always think you can be fobbed off with anything. Cold food, lousy service. Not that I often eat out. Can't afford to, for one thing, but chiefly because I hate being cheated. Lemon sole pretending to be Dover sole, that sort of thing. And made-up dishes are often horse meat!'

George looked down at his plate of *bœuf bourguignonne* and shuddered a little. 'I think you're safe enough here.'

'Oh, it all *looks* very nice. But one might feel differently if one saw the kitchen! And the expensive places are often the worst. That's well known!'

'I often eat here,' George said. 'I think it's really quite clean.'

She shook her head, smiling knowledgeably. 'Men don't notice things. Just look at my hand.'

She held it out, palm upwards. There was a dark mark across her fingers. 'Silver polish. They didn't wash the forks properly after they'd cleaned them. I suppose they think, if they keep the lights dim, they'll get away with that sort of thing.'

'I'm sorry,' George said. 'I'll ask for a clean fork when the waiter comes back. And a finger bowl for your hand.'

She stared at him. Then put her hand out of sight, in her lap. She sighed and said softly, 'I'm sorry, I'm *sorry*. I haven't been out for so long. I was looking forward to it so much, I can't tell you. I'm behaving like a silly child, cross because the marvellous treat isn't perfect! And it's not even that. The meat was all right. I don't know why I did it! What gets into me!'

Her huge eyes were very dark in the lamplight; a deep, sexual blue. Her voice was desolate. 'Oh, that's a lie. I know what it is. Why I acted like that! I have this terrible, compulsive need to make things go wrong. Because once they've *gone* wrong, once you've ruined everything, hit bottom, so to speak, you know the worst and you can't be hurt anymore.' She smiled at him sadly. 'I've been hurt so often that I'm afraid to be happy. I *was* so happy, getting ready to go out this evening, that it frightened me. I looked at my face in the mirror and thought – oh, you *fool*! And as we drove here and came in and sat down, I got more and more frightened. I suppose I thought – this is far too good to last, so let's put a stop to it now, and get it over with! Oh, not *consciously* – some idiotic, trembling little creature inside of me . . .'

She laughed breathlessly. Eased by confession, her face seemed to grow plumper and smoother. She looked very pretty. 'There. It's out now My dreadful secret. You must think me so silly.'

'Only honest,' George said. 'Rather honest and brave.'

He said this to Claire. She said, 'George, you're being perverse.'

'I don't think so.'

He was helping Claire make coffee in her kitchen, putting delicate, hand-painted cups onto a lacquer tray. Claire reached up to a cupboard and brought down four crystal glasses. As she carefully placed them, one by one on the tray, she handled them with obvious, slow, sensual pleasure and, for a moment, her face became unfamiliar to George, long-nosed, crafty; he saw her as a shallow stranger, a spoiled, rich woman, defined and identified and secured by her possessions.

He said, 'Leila's had a wretched life. At least, by our standards. It takes courage, don't you think, to admit it? And unusual honesty?'

Claire shrugged her shoulders, smirking at something; some derogatory thought.

He said, more sharply, 'She has no money, she has a boring job, she hates living alone . . .'

'George, darling! Is there *no* shelter on the blasted heath?' Claire laughed, swinging her shining hair back, inviting him to laugh with her. When he didn't, she looked reproachful, then gently forgiving. 'I'm sorry if you think I'm unfeeling. But don't let yourself be blackmailed, you silly, soft fool! You're not responsible.'

'I know that. And I don't feel it.'

He thought he had only felt flattered by Leila's obvious need. But as he carried the tray upstairs into the drawing-room, he heard her say to Sam, 'George thinks there may be something in this Buddhist business,' and was startled by the painful anxiety he felt for her.

He put the tray down, carefully avoiding Sam's eye, and said brightly, acting the life and soul of the party, 'What are you doing, young Leila, taking my name in vain?'

She looked at him gratefully. She had done her best to carry the social burden in his absence but had found it heavy. 'It's what *I* think, really. I was just trying to give my humble opinion more weight!'

Sam and Claire laughed and George felt proud and relieved, like a parent whose child has shown it is not quite defenceless.

'I mean, if this life isn't much fun, it's a comfort to hope the next may be better.'

Sam smiled at her. 'It's a sweet thought. It reminds me of something our old headmaster used to say, during religious instruction. Do you remember, George?'

'The love of God is a splendid thing. Awfully nice and jolly.'

Leila lifted her eyebrows. 'What a peculiar thing to say. Was it meant to be funny?'

Sam and George groaned in unison.

'I don't think so,' Claire said. 'Apparently this man often made remarks of this kind. Sam and George treasure them. We don't have to.'

Leila said gaily, 'Little things please little minds.'

'You could put it that way.' Claire's mouth twitched, very slightly.

She poured coffee. Sam rose to offer liqueurs. He said, to Leila, 'What's your poison?' – a phrase he never used normally and only used now, it seemed to George, because he imagined it might be her idiom. But perhaps Sam meant nothing, no social judgement; was only tired, or uneasy.

Leila said, 'It must be marvellous, being a doctor. A really worthwhile job. I do wish I had a vocation.'

She had been nervous earlier but had relaxed now. Smiling as if, since she had made them laugh, she could trust them to like her. George saw Sam look at Claire and knew what they really thought, and felt angry. He felt estranged from his old friends, whom he cared about much more than he cared about this pretty, silly, middle-aged woman, but they didn't need him as she did. He caught her eye and smiled to encourage her and then felt self-conscious because Claire was watching them with a sly expression of private amusement.

George tried not to look at her, but while Sam spoke of his job, to please Leila, he was aware of Claire sitting there, nose sharp with contempt, and resentment began to build up in him. Not from scratch but building on something already there; something that he had, until now, tried not to acknowledge.

Leila said, 'It surprises me, really, that George isn't a doctor. Or something like that. A professional man.'

Claire snorted with laughter.

Sam said, 'Oh, George thinks he has a superior vocation. And he has, in a way. The best prescription for most people is often a holiday.'

Leila looked perplexed. 'Well, I suppose you could see it like that.'

'It's the way *I* see it,' George said. 'I'll tell you why, if you like.'

He looked directly at Claire; one brief, blinding look. She smiled and lowered her eyes to her lap.

Chapter 3

Leila said, 'I don't think Claire really liked you telling that story. I'm afraid she thought it wasn't in very good taste.'

'Is that what you think Claire thought? Or is it your own opinion?'

She laughed, flustered. 'Oh, you're teasing me, aren't you? Well, to be honest, I suppose I didn't think it was very *nice*. But she looked really quite shocked!'

'I can't imagine why she should be.'

'Perhaps it's more of a *man's* story. Sam seemed to see the funny side, anyway.' She paused, smiling; she felt she had been a success with Sam. 'He's nice, isn't he? Such a *masculine* man.'

In Sam's company, George had looked frail, almost girlish. A grandmother's rather than a mother's boy; gentle, clean, and polite. Tall and slender beside that strong, stocky frame. Sam adored rugger, was constantly fighting, perpetually grubby.

But they were always together. The attraction of opposites, George's grandmother said. She was an innocent woman and meant nothing by this.

Sam came to puberty earlier. He was a man with a deep voice in a class of fluting thirteen-year-olds. He was summoned, with older boys, to the headmaster's study for a talk about sex. He reported him as approaching the subject by saying, 'My wife sometimes troubles me in the spring.' But for some days afterwards he was oddly quiet, almost surly.

His mother had to go into hospital and he came to stay with George for a week. They shared George's single bed, talking until either his mother or his grandmother rapped on the wall, and then sleeping comfortably together all night like spoons in a drawer. One morning, George woke early and woke Sam by wrestling with him, half in play, half stirred by his friend's close warm body. Sam responded; for a few minutes they wriggled together like puppies. Then Sam pushed George away and jumped out of bed. He said roughly, 'Oh, for Christ's sake, don't start *that*.'

Sam was brick-red with shame. The headmaster had said other things that he hadn't passed on. George knew this without being told, without really understanding; only an unformed idea at the back of his mind. For some time he was careful not to touch Sam, turned his back in the changing room after games, forced himself to repeat dirty jokes about girls. He looked up the word 'homosexual' in the dictionary and worried in secret. And at the end of the year, when they had to decide what subjects to concentrate on, he chose history and modern languages because Sam chose the Sciences.

Sam knew exactly what he had done. Like many tough-seeming boys, he was exceptionally sensitive. A velvet fist inside an iron glove. He tried to make up for it. When they larked about with girls, in the park or at the coffee-bar, he would warn them, 'You watch out for friend George. He's a bloody *sex-maniac*.'

They remained very close friends; grew up together, David and Jonathan, George's innocent grandmother said. But the incident stayed with George: perhaps because Sam had been right, if only for that one, passing moment, it was burned into his memory, a permanent scar. And when Claire wept in his arms, that wet day at Oxford, the thought came into his mind: *that 'ud show him! That would teach him a lesson!'*

A ludicrous reaction, of course! He wouldn't have acted upon it. He was always amused by the sly madness behind much human behaviour but he would never have slept with Sam's wife for such a ridiculous, inadmissible reason. But he did love Claire; beautiful, good, laughing Claire. And Sam, too. *Poor Sam* – that was another thought! As Leila said, 'Such a masculine man.'

Leila said, 'Was it *true*, George?'

Very briefly, George considered answering her honestly. He had taken her home; was sitting, now, on a tightly upholstered, uncomfortable sofa in her small flat, drinking instant coffee. But she had only asked out of surface curriosity; her question prompted by a desperate need to appear constantly arresting, radiantly alert, and so what he said was, 'More or less, I suppose. I mean, I've repeated this story so often that I can't really remember exactly what I was told at the time and what I've put into it since. You know how it is.'

'I'm afraid I don't.' She frowned, catching her lower lip fetchingly between her teeth, anxious to please, to keep him here a little longer, sitting on her sofa at a safe distance from her own person and drinking the vile beverage she had prepared for him. But although she wanted this, her nature was to test him, suggest that she wasn't taken in by his charms; drop a hint, even, that she found his whole attitude mildly despicable.

She said, 'Well, if you invented part of it, I must say it puts you in rather a peculiar light!' She giggled suddenly and girlishly and her colour rose – was this going too far? She added, quickly, 'Though perhaps all I mean is that it explains why it seems so unlikely. I mean, *you* couldn't know how a woman would really behave in a situation like that! I mean, as a woman *myself*, I really don't see how one could possibly approach the subject *quite* like that, with a man!'

'It wouldn't be much good approaching it with another woman, would it?' George said pleasantly.

Claire had said, 'I want to ask you a favour, George.'

They were alone together in Sam and Claire's room in the house in Holywell that Claire's father had bought for her. They had eaten lunch, ham and cheese and French bread and a bottle of wine, sitting on Sam and Claire's bed. Sam had eaten in college and would be playing rugger all afternoon. It was a bitter, February day; sleet rattled the windows.

George said, 'Anything, love.'

He was in love with Claire. How could he not be? She was kind, and funny, and marvellous to look at; she had thick, smooth, shining, silver-blonde hair and grey eyes and the most beautiful arms in the world. George couldn't see her arms now, because they were hidden under one of Sam's sweaters, a thick, white one, knitted in oiled wool by his mother, but if he closed his eyes he could remember what they had looked like the first time he saw them.

That was at a party in Nairobi. George had pointed her out to Sam. 'That girl,' he said, 'the one in the red dress with the lovely arms.' Although she was a very slender, small girl, her arms were smoothly rounded, smooth-skinned, smoothly brown. 'Oh *that* girl,' Sam had said, staring. Then 'Oh Christ, *yes*.' He put his drink down and went straight towards her. George followed at once, but Sam reached her first.

When the party was over, they went on to a night club where an English girl from Birmingham, billed under a Chinese name, took off her clothes to music. They had not known there was a strip turn because they had not been able to afford this kind of place before. They could afford it now because George had just sold his baby elephant pictures to *Paris Match*.

Sam was embarrassed by this Birmingham girl taking her clothes off. He sat with his back to the floor show and said afterwards, to George, 'That was bloody embarrassing. Sitting with a girl like Claire with that other girl waving her great tits about.'

George knew what he meant. Claire was an upper-class girl to be treated respectfully. He said, 'Don't be a bloody snob, Sam.'

George was not troubled by social distinctions, as Sam was. But he was impressed by Claire's confident air, her rich girl's assurance, and assumed it reflected a deep, inner certainty.

So when she said, 'I want you to give me a baby, George. Sam can't. Will you?' he was sure she was perfectly calm and collected and was ashamed of his own sweating lack of sophistication.

He got up from the bed and went to the window. He stood looking out at the February day and thought of Sam on the rugger field. He said, 'D'you mean Sam is impotent?' His tongue felt clumsy and dry in his mouth.

'No. Sub-fertile.'

'That means?'

'He could make me pregnant but it's a bit of a long shot.'

'Oh.' His eyes smarted suddenly. He blinked and said in a comic voice, 'Dear Lord above!' Then, 'Why don't you adopt a baby, then? Wouldn't Sam prefer that?'

'It's more complicated.' She made a sound that was meant to be laughter. 'You know Daddy didn't want us to marry?'

'I do recall something of the sort.'

'I got him to change his mind by saying I was pregnant. I wasn't.'

'Well?'

'Of course I told him I'd had a miscarriage. He accepted that.'

She stopped. She seemed to be waiting for him to speak but he could think of nothing to say.

She said, 'But he knows I want a baby. So he's likely to guess, if I don't get pregnant again, that I lied to him earlier. And though he'd forgive me in the end, I expect, he'd be dreadfully hurt. He loves me, you see. After Mummy died, we were always together.'

George thought he could hardly believe this. He turned from the window and saw she was crying; great, fat tears rolling down her cheeks silently. He went to sit beside her on the bed and put his arms round her.

He said, 'Are you asking me to make love to you for your *father's* sake?'

She gave a little, hiccuping moan – almost laughing. 'Not quite, George! For Sam's sake, too. Daddy doesn't like Sam but if he knew this, he'd despise him. Sam couldn't bear that!'

Sam was scared of his father-in-law. He stood six inches taller than Sam, was six foot four in his socks; a big, arrogant, successful, rich man. A great bull.

George whistled through his teeth. 'It's ridiculous.'

'That's why I was able to ask you. You're the only man I know who'd appreciate that!'

'Oh, so you think I'm ridiculous, do you? That's a bloody fine compliment.'

Her tears had dried, leaving her eyes flat and shining. She said, 'George, don't be stupid. I'm asking you to be my child's father.'

He held her at arm's length, staring at her. He was twenty years old, a young man deeply affected by women, and he was in love with this girl.

She said, 'Smile at me. I love the way you screw up your eyes when you smile.'

He sighed. 'Oh, Claire . . .'

She said, 'Don't you want me, George?'

Leila said, 'Oh, I've no doubt any man would agree to a proposition like that. I know what men are when it comes to a bit of fun and no responsibility. But it's harder to take that he just accepted the situation later on, if he cared for the woman at all. Especially once the boy was actually born. You know how men are about their sons!'

George said, 'There was nothing he could have done, was there?'

Claire went into a London teaching hospital to have her baby. George went to see her. She was in a private room, full of flowers.

He said, 'Claire darling. Darling Claire. This is a farce, isn't it? Leave Sam and marry me. Please, Claire. I love you, sweet, darling Claire.'

She said, 'I love Sam more than my life.'

He was ashamed. He sat by the bed and talked to her. He told her funny stories about the travel agency he was working for and made her laugh. He laughed himself a great deal.

Sam came in with his mother and George stood up and kissed her. He was fond of Sam's mother whom he had known since he made friends with Sam, when he first went to school. She had fed him enormous meals in her kitchen, whenever Sam brought him home, taught him to ride a bicycle, bandaged his cut knees when he was little, teased him like a kind aunt as he grew older. She was a strong-willed, happy woman; a dependable fixture in the landscape of his life.

She was also the first woman he had ever seen naked. He had been playing in Sam's back yard and had run into the house to pee. The lavatory was in the bathroom and the bathroom was on the ground floor, an extension Sam's father had built on to the kitchen. He ran in, clutching himself, and Sam's mother was standing up in the bath with her back to him. He stood there, irresolute – he was six years old – and she turned and looked down at him, smiling. She said, 'Oh, it's you, George, lucky it wasn't the milkman,' and reached out for a towel, but quite slowly (so as not to embarrass him he realized gratefully, many years later) and he had time to look at her, at her long naked back and the nobs of her spine sweeping down from the nape of her neck to the little patch of dark down just above the firm swell of her buttocks.

She had been beautiful then; dark, quick-moving and slender. She was still very handsome; tall and broad-shouldered with a proud way of carrying her head. She said, 'Well, George, isn't this an occasion!'

Sam said, 'You seen my young limb of a daughter?'

A nurse brought Sally in. She weighed six and a half pounds; was red, raw, and bawling.

Sam's mother said, 'Isn't she beautiful?'

George looked at the baby, touched the palm of one hand. She grasped his finger.

Sam's mother wept. She said, 'My first grand-daughter. Oh Sam, I wish your dad was alive, I wish he could see her. Such a beautiful baby. Isn't she beautiful? Who do you think she takes after?'

Claire said, 'She looks like Sam. Don't you think so?'

Sam laughed. 'Poor little sod, what a fate!'

Claire said in her light, cool, confident voice, 'Don't you think she looks like Sam, George?'

Leila said, 'Of course, the woman must have been the most frightful cold bitch. Poor old William Barnet. I mean, when you think of it, you can't help feeling sorry for him. To be made use of like that and then tossed aside like – like – oh, I don't know . . .'

'Like a sucked orange?' George suggested. He was amused by how excited she suddenly seemed; eyes bright, mind fizzing with all the implications of poor Barnet's story, her body softened, relaxed with the pleasures of moral indignation and vicarious sex. George looked at her, curled prettily on the floor with one arm on a chair, and knew he could have her. Did he want her? The thought stirred him agreeably. He said, 'I really ought to be going.'

She said, 'Well, that's a bit of a cliché. But it must have been awful for him. I expect she kept him hanging about, enjoying the feeling they shared a secret. Even enjoying the feeling he might give her away. Some women are like that, you know. They like a feeling of danger. The spice of life, isn't it?'

Had Claire enjoyed it? He had wondered sometimes. But she had never betrayed what she felt by a word or a look. It might have been a dream he had had! Even when he told Barnet's story she simply smiled and looked down at her lap. Accepting her punishment? That was how it might seem; was how, he supposed, he'd intended it. Not that he blamed himself. There was no point in blaming oneself, that was just self-indulgence. He didn't pretend to be saintly. Nice George. Poor old George. Well, he wasn't.

He said, 'Perhaps it was Barnet who got the most fun out of it in the end. He said so. He said he liked the feeling of power.'

Poor old Barnet! How he'd been used! He was real enough; he and George had got drunk in Rome on his eldest son's birthday. He was a lonely man, unhappy because his wife had left him. That was all. The rest was fiction.

Leila said, 'That makes him a lot less *nice*, of course. But perhaps he only told you that for pride's sake. Or as a sort of safety-valve, do you think? If you tell yourself you've got the whip hand, you're less inclined to use it.'

'It could just have been a pack of lies, of course,' George said.

How he had really felt, he could hardly remember. Some guilt, naturally. But that had been lessened by something Claire had said the first time they had made love. He had been nervous, he had only been to bed with a girl twice before: once at Oxford, after a party, and once with a tart in Nairobi. Claire was giggly in bed; funny and friendly. She said, 'Don't *worry*, George, it's not a competitive sport.' And, 'That really was awfully nice and jolly, as I expect your old headmaster would say. I must say I'm relieved. Sam once said that he wasn't *sure*, but he thought you just *might* be a queer!'

Not much guilt after that! Perhaps that was why she had said it; to ease him. Claire was deliberate in most things.

George remembered the story she had told them that first night in Nairobi. When she was fourteen, her parents had given a party. Her mother, who was alive then, had insisted that Claire was too young to attend this grown-up occasion. Claire had waited in her room until the party was well under way and then made her entrance, naked as the day she was born except for a string of pearls her father had given her. She said, 'My mother never dared send me to bed after that!'

Sam had been shocked, but admiring. George, inclined to fantasy himself, hadn't believed her; had thought she was

61

teasing Sam, or trying to relieve his obvious embarrassment over the strip-tease performance. But he believed her now; saw her behaviour was always consistent. She was used to getting what she wanted in the most direct way, even if that way was sometimes outrageous, and she did not expect to face difficulties. She had picked on George now (he sometimes thought sourly) because she knew that he loved her, and Sam, and could be trusted not to make trouble.

It was that he resented, perhaps. It made him seem negligible. Not a force to be reckoned with.

Which he wasn't, of course. It was his problem that he had no proper, solid sense of his own importance, no capacity for indignation on his own account. Oh, he had moments of bitter rage, love, resentment, but he could not accept them as dignified emotions, rightful springboards for action. He always had the feeling that he was making a fuss over nothing. Other people lived seriously, serious lives, but his own was a shadow play.

There was nothing to be done, anyway. And it wasn't so terrible. Worse things, as his grandmother often said, happened at sea. Did she ever think, when she proferred this piece of folk-wisdom as a comfort for some small disaster, of George's drowned, young father? He sometimes wondered, but thought probably not. You can read too much into chance remarks. Like Claire's, on Sally's first birthday, when she suddenly said, 'Situations that look ghastly from the outside are never as bad once you're in them.'

Had this been meant as a message for George? He couldn't remember the context, only Claire's pale, fine-boned face as she smiled up at him, her child on her knee, and the wild, answering leap of his conspirator's heart. But she had probably been talking about something else altogether. Perhaps just the whole, tiresome business of being tied down by a baby; of not being free any longer.

It was true, though. You can get used to almost anything, given time, and George had grown used to this. There were long stretches when he didn't think about it at all and others when it seemed little more than a mildly embarrassing joke. Something that fitted in perfectly with what he saw as his somewhat clownish life-style.

As Leila did, in a way. He did not intend to marry her but she was, from all points of view, such an absurd choice that he knew it was possible. Claire had been right; he was naturally perverse. Perversity was a weak man's answer to strength of purpose, perhaps. Was he weak? Strength needs an object and he had nothing he obviously wanted; the last few years he had drifted, expecting his life to change, but not sure in what way. Although he still travelled, most of the time full of hope, sometimes an immense lassitude seized him. Skimming the world's surface, as at home in Athens or Paris or Rome as he was in London, he felt oddly static; poised on the edge of his future like a nervous boy on the edge of a swimming bath.

Claire pushed him into it. Claire and Sally between them.

He took Leila to France for a late summer holiday. She had not 'had a break' as she put it, for years, and this shocked George, professionally. Unhappiness shocked him too, and he was sure she was deeply unhappy. Not just with her life; with herself. She said, 'I know that I put people off but I can't stop myself. I'm afraid I can't compromise. I suppose it's having high standards.'

She seemed proud and pleased as she said this but George was sure she was unhappy in her heart, because he would have been.

They toured the Loire valley. It was beautiful weather and she looked young and brown and rested in the sun. George

63

made no sexual advances beyond a chaste kiss when they parted each evening, but one night, in Chartres, she came to his room. She said, 'I don't know if this is what you want but it seemed only fair to make the offer.'

She was belligerent and shy. George was touched by her awkwardness. He tried to make her happy but she was as stiff as a girl who had never made love in her life. She moaned and threw herself about, energetically, and he let her think he was taken in by this act; was moved that she should pretend for his pleasure. He knew, in some part of his mind, that she would expect him to pay for it too, but he didn't resent it. She had a sense of her own value and that was something he lacked.

She said, sighing reproachfully, 'I'm afraid I'm terribly inhibited. Something inside me always holds back. I hope it didn't spoil things for you.'

He stroked her damp hair back. He said, 'You were lovely.'

She said, 'Once, on my mother's birthday, she was ill in bed and my father took her breakfast up and I came to see her open her presents. My father had bought her a green blouse and when she'd looked at it, she said, you know very well I can't wear that colour, and threw it straight at him. He flinched back and I *felt* it – as if she'd thrown something heavy at me! Sometimes I think that affected me in my sex life. I'm afraid to let myself go in case I'm rejected. Like giving someone a present and having it thrown back in your face!'

He said, 'That's a bit far-fetched, isn't it? You're not inhibited, anyway. We're just not used to each other.'

He began to kiss her again. She squirmed away and said in an indignant voice, 'I don't see why you think that's far-fetched! The oddest things affect people. Cripple them permanently! And that incident must have affected me or I wouldn't have thought of it now!'

Her eyes were dark pools staring up at him sadly and angrily. She gave a short, wounded laugh and said, 'Oh, I'm sorry. I've no business to bore you with my dreary psychological hang-ups. That's not what you bargained for, is it? It's not even as if you could do anything about them.'

'How do you know I can't?' George said. He felt very penitent.

When they got back from France, he invited Sam and Claire out to dinner. He thought it would be easier for Leila to meet them on neutral ground. It was partly the burden of being always in social debt that made her treat the world with such freezing disdain. And she did seem happier in the restaurant than she usually was in other people's houses, sipping her martini without complaint, even though it had lemon in it, and talking about their holiday openly and naturally as if she had actually enjoyed herself and, for once, saw no weakness or danger in admitting this. She was a little proprietary, saying 'we' all the time. 'We' thought that. 'We' did this. And making their relationship clear, 'Do you remember those ducks at that little pub near Rouen, George? We thought we'd found such a quiet place, off the road, and they started up about three in the morning and kept us awake for the rest of the night!'

Claire listened to every word she spoke with exaggerated attention. Her polite smiles and gracious questions filled the restaurant with gusts of icy air. Fortunately, only George and Sam noticed.

When the two women had gone to the cloakroom at the end of the meal, Sam said, 'That was a jolly display of territorial aggro, wasn't it? Don't take too much notice of Claire, old boy. You know what women are like with bachelor friends of the family. They get used to having an unattached man around. Useful, like a spare tyre.'

'Thank you.'

Sam looked thoughtfully into the dregs of his decaffeinated coffee. 'Mind you, I'd be sorry to see you rush into anything. Though it's none of my business. But as Claire said – old George doesn't realize it, but he's a considerable catch, money-wise.'

He laughed, apologetically.

'Claire said that?' To Claire, money was a natural element, like air or water; not something to be discussed or considered.

'Well, no. Sally did, actually. She gets her vulgarity from me. She said, is George going to marry that cat-woman? Tell him she's after his money.'

This was partly a joke, partly not. Sam added quickly, 'I said to her, your Uncle George is a big boy, he can look after himself.'

'Good of you,' George said 'How is Sally?' A polite enquiry as if he were asking after one of Sam's distant relations.

'Fine, I hope.' Sam pulled a wry face. 'You keep your fingers crossed with a girl that age, it's all you can do. But she got on well with that cousin of his Omer sent us. Or his cousin's cousin – I'm not sure what the relationship is. Fairly distant, I think. Certainly Zeynep hasn't seen him for years – her parents live in New York and she's still at school there. But she's going to Turkey, either next summer or the one after – it's not settled yet – and we hope Sal will go with her then. Do you remember Zeynep's parents? Omer said, when he wrote, that he thought you might . . .'

He grinned at George with shame-faced relief: this was a less awkward topic than Leila.

'I didn't, until Omer reminded me,' George said. 'I met her mother at Omer's father's house, actually – oh, about ten years ago. Or eleven, perhaps. *Not* a merry occasion. Her husband was in prison. I don't remember the exact ins-and-outs of it, but he was anti-Menderes. He was released of course, when the Army overthrew the Democratic Party in 1960 and hanged Menderes. Then he went to America.'

Omer's father's house in Istanbul. Omer's father; a big man with a black beard and bright eyes, who had been a friend of Atatürk's. Omer, trying to explain the complications of Turkish politics and himself, ten years younger, too appalled and embarrassed by the family scene he had unwittingly blundered in on, to listen. A plump, dark-eyed woman, weeping. Zeynep's father had been arrested that morning. A small girl, watching her mother with a dumb, closed-in, frightened look . . .

Sam said, 'How dreadful.'

'Prison is a fairly common hazard in Turkey if you dabble in politics. Zeynep's father was an academic of some kind and left wing, though not very extreme. You didn't need to be extremist to annoy Menderes. I think I saw Zeynep too, on the same occasion. She'd have been about seven or eight. What's she like now?'

'An imposing young woman. Rather alarming, I found her. Looks you straight in the eye and finds you wanting! Lacking in moral fibre or something! I was afraid Sal would find her a bit solemn and elderly but they were thick as thieves from the word go, and she's been a good influence, I would think. Whipped Sally off to lectures and picture galleries – a glutton for cultural punishment. I must say, I was relieved though. Sal had been running wild for a month or two, hanging round coffee-bars, coming in all hours of the night. Hell of a worry – worried *me* anyway! Claire took it calmly enough, but I couldn't. She's so bloody innocent but she looks like a tramp. I suppose all fathers are sensitive about that sort of thing.'

'Yes,' George said. 'Yes, I suppose so.'

Sam looked at him. 'She's a bit hurt that you've not been to see us. She asked me to tell you.'

67

'I'm sorry,' George said. 'Tell her I'm sorry, but I've been pretty busy.'

Sally telephoned him at the end of November. She wanted to see him. She said, 'You forgot my *birthday*.'

He hadn't forgotten. He said, 'I didn't forget but I didn't know what you wanted.'

'You could have sent me a card. But I don't want a present. I want to see you.'

He met her in the tea-room at the Tate Gallery. She had come straight from her drama class; was wearing patched jeans and a sleeveless gingham smock over a faded sweater with holes in the elbows. Bare, grubby feet in thonged sandals. She said, 'I had to see you on your own. Without my parents or that ghastly woman.'

He ignored that. 'Any special reason?'

She shook her head. Her hair was longer than he remembered it. She had parted it in the middle and looked like a Pre-Raphaelite madonna. She said in a forlorn voice, 'You always used to be there and suddenly you weren't anymore. I've missed you.'

She had grown taller and narrower at the waist. Her face had beautiful hollows under the cheekbones. She had plucked her eyebrows and pencilled in new ones, a darker colour than her hair.

George said, 'I'm sorry love, I've been busy.'

'So my father said. He passed on your message.'

'I'm sorry you missed me. Though it's flattering, too.'

'Don't laugh at me or I'll kill you.'

'I wasn't laughing.'

She looked down at her hands and sighed heavily.

He said, 'Your nails are filthy.'

'I've been busy too. You're not the only person who's busy.'

He tried to make her laugh. 'I make time to wash.'

She pushed her hands between her thighs and said, 'I've been having a bloody awful time. An absolutely fucking awful time.'

'Please don't use that word,' George said.

'Why ever not? People *do* it all the time, don't they?'

'All right. Don't use it as an adjective, then. To please me. Pander to the puritan prejudices of an old-fashioned, elderly Uncle.'

'Oh, don't be so fucking stupid.'

He said, 'If you say that once more I'll get up and go,' and realized, with horror, that he was squabbling with her as if they were equals. Silly kids the same age.

He said, 'No of course I won't. That *was* stupid. I'm sorry, Sally. I'm sorry I haven't been to see you. But when I did come to the house, you weren't there. And I really have been enormously busy. I went to Greece and Turkey in May and June, and to France in September. The rest of the time slipped away. As you get older it seems to go faster.'

She smiled, slightly and sadly.

He said, 'What have you been doing with yourself? Sam told me you had a nice summer with Zeynep. Showing her London.'

She shrugged her shoulders.

'But I expect that seems ages ago. Are you having a good term at school?'

She looked at him with such utter misery that he felt sick and breathless.

He said, 'Sally. Sally, darling. Are you in some sort of trouble?'

'What sort do you mean?'

'I don't know. Any sort.'

She said, 'I'm not on drugs. The police aren't after me. I'm not pregnant.' She assumed a mock-cockney accent. 'I've bin to the Clinic and I takes me pills regular.'

He felt as if some large hand had picked him up by the scruff of his neck and dropped him down from a height.

She said, 'Do me a favour. Don't say, *Oh Sally!*'

'It's not my business, of course. But since you've told me, I think I'm entitled to comment. Does your mother know?'

She rolled her eyes. She had gone rather pink. 'Oh be your *age*, Uncle George.'

'I'm trying to be.' He was trying. But what he wanted to do was wave his arms about, go red in the face, stamp and shout, '*Who's the man?*' Get out his horse-whip!

She was breathing more easily. 'I haven't told her because she'd tell *Dad*. She'd see it as sensible but he'd think it was a moral issue.'

'Yes, he would.'

George thought about this. Sam was a practising Christian. A Methodist. George had a sudden, sharp memory of meeting Sam one Sunday morning; himself on his bicycle, waving at the little, square-faced boy trotting along beside his tall, handsome mother, both holding their Bibles, and feeling an odd, shy, wondering shame, as if he had inadvertently spied on his friend. Although they had never discussed it, George knew that Sam's faith informed his life. Sam had never gone to bed with a girl before Claire. But apart from that, what did religion amount to? A belief in some basic, psychic unity between people, a holding to certain fixed principles? A comfort, a sweet, private ease – and in this case, a protection! Ignorance could be bliss – Lord, as you grew older, how the truth of old clichés came thundering home! One respected beliefs one didn't share. Sam would be spared this anguish, this tearing, animal rage ...

Sally said, 'Morals don't come into it. Only for people like Dad.'

'Well. But there's a medical side, too. There are dangers. Your father would know more about that than I do.'

'They're exaggerated.'

He said, feeling his way, 'You're not very old, after all.' Under-age, surely? Sixteen now, but she'd spoken as if this had gone on for some time. How had she got a prescription? Lied probably. He didn't want to know.

She said, 'If I could grow older faster, I would.'

They were sitting in the corner of the restaurant, drinking coffee. There was a pair of middle-aged ladies at the next table. No, not middle-aged. His own age. Out of earshot but watching with pleasure this young and beautiful girl talking so intently with a fatherly gentleman. One of them caught his eye and smiled.

He said, 'I suppose everyone wants to grow up. Perhaps it's sentimental of older people to think it a pity to hurry the process.'

'You know why I want to.'

He understood suddenly. She was Claire's daughter. Claire would do anything to get her own way. Sally was ruthless, like her mother. He drew a deep breath. He was helpless.

Sally said, 'I am grown up, really. In some countries, I'd be married with two children already. It's simply a question of social attitudes. But I'm not a child, even here.'

'You are to me.' The truth of this struck him.

She said, 'You're not so much older than I am.'

'Twenty odd years.'

She went on, sturdily, 'You're young for your age. You look at least ten years younger than Dad. And I'm old for mine.'

He looked at her. She was Claire's daughter. But she was Sally. And miserable. He longed to put his arms round her. Desire made him sick.

She was rosy-red now. She said, 'I've put it all badly. I've made you angry. I'm sorry. I just wanted to make you see I

71

really was old enough. To make you look at me differently.'

Relief came flooding in like a tide. So she had made all this up! She was showing off. The pill was a status symbol. Schoolgirls swapped them like sweets. Perhaps this was true, perhaps not. It was the way he intended to look at it.

He said, 'Let's get out of here, if you've finished your coffee. It isn't a suitable place for this conversation.'

He waited while she went to the cloakroom. He thought – I could go! But he waited and she came up the stairs, running. She had put on an embroidered, leather coat with a long, rough, fur lining. She smelt like a wet goat.

They walked along the Embankment. A white mist rose from the river, like steam, Her hair was covered with pearly drops. She put her arm through his, hugging close to his side, and he thought – I shall never be so happy again in my life!

He cleared his throat. He said, 'Listen, Sally. Sally darling, listen to me. I love you dearly, you should know that, and I don't want . . .'

'But,' she said. '*But*. Don't go on, *Uncle* George. Not with that speech, anyway.'

'I can't make any other, my pet.'

She jerked her arm roughly away and looked up at him. 'All right. But don't tell me bloody *lies*, then. You don't love me, that's *all*.' Her eyes were shining, either with the damp, or with tears. But her mouth smiled. She said, in a croaky voice, 'Don't you even fancy me? Just a little bit? It would be enough to be going on with, for me. I'm not ugly, am I?'

He looked at her. She was a heartless bitch. A sad child. His darling.

He said, 'Of course you're not ugly. But if you want the truth, I really prefer older women.'

She went on smiling. She would smile like that, he thought, if he'd hit her.

She said, 'Okay. Okay I asked for that, didn't I? At least you can't say I didn't try.'

'No indeed,' he said. 'Full marks for trying.'

She nodded. 'Thank you. Now, if you don't mind . . .' Her smile wavered briefly, then she hitched it firmly back into place. 'If you don't mind, Uncle George, I think I'll go now. Perhaps you'd be frightfully kind and give me a bit of a start.'

He nodded. He was speechless. She turned, flipping her hand up in a farewell. He watched her leave him, half running, half walking, long, damp hair flying behind like the tail of a smart little pony. He felt a hollow weakness inside, as if from internal bleeding; his life, trickling out.

When she was almost out of sight, she turned back and shouted, 'Uncle George! Don't forget my birthday present. Next time you go abroad. A doll, or a toy drum, or something.'

Chapter 4

When he told his grandmother he was marrying Leila and she said, 'But George, she's older than you,' he answered, with genuine surprise, 'Only four years.'

Compared with twenty, this age gap seemed nothing.

After Sally had left him on the Embankment, he had walked for several hours, through swirling fog, castigating himself, building up a picture in his mind of a leering, elderly satyr, dragging up from the depths of his memory endless occasions when he had embraced her with false, jolly heartiness, or simply sat looking at her, doting like a kindly uncle but enjoying, all the time, what seemed now a monstrous sexual pleasure. Monstrous, because he had persuaded himself that his knowledge of their real relationship made this indulgence entirely innocent, forgetting that she might see it differently, put a different interpretation on his sly, approving glances, his old man's lust.

Oh – he had cheated her doubly. As a father, as a lover. A deceit all the more abominable because he had slipped into it so easily over the years that it had come to seem quite natural, not a crime at all. But it had been criminal to ignore the rule that all actions must, in the end, have a consequence; to be blind to the laws of causality. His only defence was that he had been very young but that was no defence. Still less to blame Claire, younger still.

Poor Sally. Poor child, poor bird. Although it was all drama, possibly. That was not a criticism of her. It was natural for a girl to flirt with an old friend of the family; try out her young wings. A simulated emotion was healthy at her age; a dry run at the real thing. If it was a dry run. He thought – Juliet was fourteen—and had a moment of aching longing and loss. Not in his loins, in his heart. A burning pain in his chest. Indigestion, he thought, and laughed. What was love, after all? A similar biological function; a trick to keep the race going.

He didn't believe this. He stopped on Westminster Bridge and shouted aloud. 'Sally, Sally ...' Her name boomed mournfully back, distorted and hollow-sounding, as if the fog were a wall or a tunnel. A uniformed figure appeared out of the mist and hesitated beside him. The policeman said, 'Are you all right, Sir?'

'Quite all right, Officer.' But further reassurance seemed needed. He smiled agreeably and said, 'Just testing the echo.'

The policeman smiled back doubtfully. He was young, with a chubby chin framed by the strap of his helmet. A young, plump policeman on Westminster Bridge, wondering if this tired man in expensive, shabby clothes, might be going to jump. But it was only a despairing old goat, in love with his daughter.

His age was an indictment. But it was also a refuge. All passion spent – or if it wasn't spent yet, he knew it would pass. Did *she* know it would? Perhaps not, his poor love, but she would find out quite soon. You judge people by the company they keep. When he was married to Leila she would look at the pair of them and be disgusted, perhaps. A disgusting old couple. A comfortable, middle-aged pair.

His grandmother said, 'Well, I suppose you know what you're doing,' but he saw that it did not greatly concern her. Since her eightieth birthday she had slipped, quite suddenly, into very old age; a symptom, it seemed, more of resignation than physical decline, as if she had made some private, internal decision to let go. Always a gentle woman, she now seemed totally passive and accepting, uninterested in anything beyond her own, mercifully small, aches and pains, and the characters in several serials she watched daily on television; hardly aware of the continuing existence of anyone in the real world, except perhaps Elspeth.

Now she said, 'You know Elspeth has a bad cough,' speaking reproachfully as if by intruding on her peace with this small matter of his marriage he had somehow diminished the importance of Elspeth's health.

He knew Elspeth was ill. He had found her one morning, retching desperately into the kitchen sink. She had raised her head, still helmeted with those strange, metallic, chrysanthemum curls, and said, 'It looks as if your grandma and I are going to be a sodding photo-finish. Though I'm going the hard way. With luck she'll just drift off one day when she's ready, like a puff of bloody thistle-down.'

He said to his grandmother, 'Elspeth smokes too much, darling.'

'That's what Leila says. She comes here and she runs round opening the windows and shaking the curtains. There's no need for it. I like the smell of cigars.'

The room stank, Leila said. A meticulous housekeeper, she was always plumping up cushions and emptying ashtrays. When she visited his grandmother, she couldn't resist tidying up a bit. 'Poor old soul, I can't bear to see her living in such a mess. She ought to have someone living in, really. You're rich enough, George. That dreadful Elspeth doesn't even keep the place clean. Cobwebs and dust and rings on the furniture – I told her the other day that there's some new stuff on the market that's good for removing those horrid white stains but she just stared as if she'd never heard the words furniture polish! As if I were speaking some strange foreign language!'

George's grandmother said, 'She upsets Elspeth.'

'She only means to be kind.'

She looked at him doubtfully. 'As long as you're happy.'

He expected to be. Hoped to achieve this, in part, by making Leila happier than she had been up to now. She had not had much luck and it had made her narrow and watchful; perpetually on guard against the next blow. But people could change and he was sure he could change her; coax her, with kindness, out of the chilly fortress of anger from which she surveyed the world.

He enjoyed the challenge; flexed his crusader's muscles. He was not being altruistic. He was marrying her for his own reasons which were not particularly admirable. One reason was that she was the last woman to make him feel guilty because he had made use of her. When he proposed she gave him a bleak, angry stare and said, 'I suppose you think I ought to be grateful.' And although a moment later she was sobbing in his arms, his relief was so great he could almost believe that he loved her. He felt such respect for her absurd, spiky honesty. She was comic and touching. Drying her tears and blowing her nose on his handkerchief, she said, 'I'm my own worst enemy but at least I do know it.'

Perhaps he did love her. There are many gradations. You couldn't expect passion at his time of life.

He said so to Sam. Sam shouted with laughter. 'For God's sake man, you're not *sixty*.'

They were standing in an upstairs room of a cottage Sam was thinking of buying. It was a few miles from George's house, outside the town. Sam had lunched with George and they had driven here together, this dark, winter afternoon. 'We'll be able to see a bit more of each other,' Sam said. 'See my mother, too. She's a touch arthritic, doesn't get out as much as she used to.'

George prodded the wood of the window sill with his penknife. Dry flakes fell to the floor. He said, 'Needs a lot of repair, doesn't it?'

'An investment, though. And it'll be nice to get out of town at weekends.'

George looked gloomily out at the untidy garden. 'Lot of work there. Half of those fruit trees are dead, did you notice?'

'Do me good. Fresh air. Exercise.' Sam patted his stomach, pushed the window open and breathed deeply. He was as excited as a child with a toy; this would be the first house he would own. The London house had been bought by Claire's father, put in Claire's name. Sam said, 'I thought I might get young Sally a horse. There's a decent sized paddock.'

'Would she like that?' Just to hear her name spoken made George feel faintly sick. 'I wouldn't have thought she was much of a country girl.'

'All girls like horses. Though she's not too keen on the cottage idea. Not on buying it, anyway. She's on a left-wing kick at the moment. Property's theft, money's disgusting, that sort of thing. *A la lanterne* with the industrialists as well as the aristos.'

'You used to think like that. We both did. I still do, sometimes.'

'We didn't want revolution though, only reform. And I must say I find Sally and her lot a bit comic. Rich young virgins, sitting around in their comfortable houses, yapping about the overthrow of society in privileged voices. Daddy's little darlings – wasn't that what Morin called

78

them? That French chap. Pretending they're in the same boat as the Workers. Quoting Chairman Mao. Oh God, oh Montreal! They don't know a bloody thing.'

'Not their fault, exactly. And I'd have thought it was healthy, at their age.'

'I suppose she'll grow out of it.'

'I didn't know she'd grown *into* it.' George laughed artificially. 'I haven't seen her – oh, for at least a couple of months. I can't exactly remember but it was long before Christmas. We didn't talk about politics.'

'Oh, she's changed quite a bit.' Sam frowned, as if he had only just realized this.

'Has she?' George felt like a ham actor with a bad script. His mouth had dried up. Any moment now Sam would turn and accuse him. An outraged father. He said, 'In what way?'

'Oh, I dunno.' Sam prowled round the room, whistling between his teeth. He put a hand thoughtfully on a damp bulge in the outer wall, squinted up at the ceiling, opened a cupboard. A pile of yellowing newspapers fell out on the uneven floor. Sam grunted as he bent to push them back. 'God, I'm out of condition. Smells a bit, doesn't it? Down there, in the corner?'

George poked his head into the cupboard and sniffed. 'Bit of dry rot, perhaps. You're bound to get that, but it's curable. You'll have to get a good surveyor. In what way has she changed?'

'Hard to put a finger on. Just growing up, I suppose. Sometimes I think what she wants is a husband and children. Daft, of course, at her age. Still. D'you know that poem? Dum-de-dum-dum – *were this wild thing wedded . . .*'

'Meredith,' George said. 'Love in a Valley. Or is it *the* valley? I can't remember.'

'Doesn't matter. You know what I mean then.'

'*Heartless she is as a shadow in the meadows?*'

'No, not that. Young Sal's not heartless. Too much heart, if anything. I don't know if it's a good poem or not, haven't read any poetry since school, but it expresses something about young girls you don't realize until you watch one growing up. They have this tremendous – what-do-you-call-it – *yearning*, I suppose, to be loved and possessed. It goes beyond sexuality, or you feel that it does. There was a day I came into a room and saw her, standing at the window and staring out – I felt it then. I can't really describe it. It wasn't long ago. Just before she went off to Switzerland, this Christmas.'

'*Sweet is her shape but sweeter unpossessed*,' George quoted. He thought that if this conversation continued much longer he would be physically sick. He said, 'Victorian sentimentality. Or morbidity. A sort of death-wish.'

'Maybe. But it twists the guts up.' Sam sighed. 'Oh, well.' He went to the window and stood, looking out at the darkening day, shoulders drooping a little. Then said, in a different voice, 'Well, you'll see for yourself.'

'What d'you mean?'

George stood beside him. The long cottage garden glimmered greyly with old man's beard, silken tassels tangled over bare trees and the brittle stalks of last summer's flowers. A dead landscape with a dead moon rising above it. Beyond the high hedge, in the lane, he could see the roof of the car they had come in, and the top of another car, drawn up behind.

Sam said, 'Claire said she might drive her Pa down. I think Sally's with her.'

They could hear women's voices. Claire was laughing. She came in at the gate and stopped to release a bramble that caught at her coat. Her father's bulk filled the path behind her. Then he bent, to help Claire, and George saw the two girls beyond him.

He said, 'Who's she got with her?'

'Zeynep. Didn't I tell you? She flew over to go ski-ing with Sal. Last minute impulse – there's money there, as they say. She's stopping with us for a few days before she goes home.'

The girls pushed past Claire and ran towards the house, looking up at the window. They wore jeans and old-fashioned, square-shouldered, fur jackets. George drew back, out of sight. He wanted to run. But there was no escape: he had come in Sam's car. Oh, for God's sake, he thought, be your *age*.

The front door was open. As Sam leant from the window, began speaking to Claire, George listened to the clatter of feet on the stairs. They seemed shod with something more solid than leather; both girls were wearing, in fact, wooden clogs. He looked at their feet as they came in the room, then raised his eyes slowly.

Sally's face was glossy brown and bare of make-up except for her eyelids, which were painted purple and decorated with what looked like small sequins at the corners. She said, 'Hi, Uncle George!' She crossed the room and stood in front of him but didn't offer her face to be kissed. He was grateful and sorry. He said, 'Hallo there! You stink of moth balls.'

She laughed and twirled round, displaying her fur coat. The contrast between the smelly antiquity of this ridiculous garment and her young, shining face, took his breath away. She said, 'We bought them on Friday in Kensington Market, aren't they *fantastic*?'

He couldn't tell whether her painted eyes were excited or nervous. He said, 'Whatever animal it came from must have died a long time ago.' He smiled at the other girl. 'I hear you've been ski-ing together.'

Sally was speaking. Introducing her friend, he supposed; all he seemed able to hear was a strange drumming inside his

81

own head as if he were drowning. Zeynep didn't answer his smile. She gave him her smooth, cool, rather large hand and appeared to look through him. She was as tall as Sally but heavier built; a strong-bodied girl with good features and light, tea-coloured eyes.

Sally said, 'We've had a simply fantastic time. God, it was bloody marvellous! Mountains and sun and snow – I simply can't *tell* you.'

'I'm glad,' George said, not looking at her. It seemed kinder even though, unlike him, she had presumably been prepared for this meeting. He realized he was still holding the Turkish girl's hand. He released it and she let it fall limply as if quite exhausted by this social necessity. He said, 'You won't remember me but we have met before. In Istanbul, a long time ago. Before your parents went to America.'

Her expression suggested both boredom and scorn. Or perhaps she was shy. He said, 'I'm a friend of Omer's. I saw you at his father's house, with your mother.'

'Oh. Really?' Her eyelids drooped as she spoke: it had been a tedious effort to respond to this irrelevant statement. George looked at her doubtfully. Something bothered him; not just her world-weary look.

Sally said, 'She's going to university in Istanbul in the autumn, isn't that super? Her parents wanted her to go to Vassar, or some crummy place like that, but she's *insisted* on going to Turkey. She can *do* so much there. Real women's lib – not just potty, bra-burning stuff! It really is frightful, some of the things that go on. She's been telling me. Did you know, in the country, some of the peasants don't even register their girls when they're born, so they won't have to go to school and can be kept working, at home, in the fields. Beasts of burden . . .'

Claire said, 'Oh Sal, not *again*, we had that lecture at lunch. George knows about the position of women in

Turkey and I'm sure he deplores it as much as you do. How are you, George darling?'

She and her father had come in together. Claire's father had to stoop to get through the doorway; even in the room, the ceiling was too low for him. He stood, heavy head bent, one huge arm round Claire's shoulders, sweaty, ruddy face smiling. Claire was smiling too; she glowed, as she always did when her father was with her, nestling in the shelter of his arm. They looked, to George at that moment, more like lovers than father and daughter. He was appalled by this thought which had come into his head, uninvited. He said, 'How are you, sir?'

'Pleased to see you, George.' Claire's father spoke with meaningful emphasis. He adored his daughter, his golden girl, and was indulgent to women in general, but preferred masculine company. And he felt particularly at ease with George because he made money rather than earned it. Men who lived on a weekly wage or a monthly salary, unless it was very large indeed, were beings from another planet to Claire's father, and made him uneasy.

Sam said, 'George is getting married. He's just told me. To Leila.'

A glance passed between him and Claire. She said instantly, 'George, I'm so glad. I do hope you'll be *enormously* happy.'

She came to kiss him, eyes tenderly bright, cool lips soft on his cheek. Her delight seemed only fractionally exaggerated; held, to George's sensitive ear, a certain apologetic relief. From guilt, over the years, or some nearer concern? Had she guessed about Sally? He forced himself to look over Claire's shoulder at her daughter and smile. She said, 'Congratulations, Uncle George,' not bravely, but blank-faced and casually as if she felt very little; certainly no shock, no humiliation. Perhaps she didn't, he thought.

She had got over it, why not? She was only a child. Last November, in a child's time-scale, was light years away. A distant memory by now; mildly embarrassing but no more. She had probably been in love ten times since . . .

His mind accepted this gratefully; his body replied with a deep, burning anguish. He said, to Claire's father, who had taken Claire's place and was pumping his hand up and down like a piece of machinery, 'Well, what do you think of the cottage? Not much room to swing a cat, I daresay, but then who wants to swing cats?'

Sam said, 'It wasn't the sort of occupation I had in mind exactly. But it's not a bad size as far as rooms are concerned. Two downstairs, and the kitchen, and four up. Though we'll have to use one for a bathroom, of course.'

Claire's father said, 'Bit on the small side for me. But whatever you buy, you can't go wrong with the property boom as it is at the moment. You have to reckon a price rise of eight per cent to make it worth while and houses are going up a good deal faster than that. What's the asking price?'

'Just under eight thousand.'

'There you are. Put a bathroom in, re-wire the place, and you'll double the value. Quite a good, small investment.' Peanuts to him, of course. But he nodded kindly at Sam, stretching his mind to see the little man's point of view. 'Make more overnight, you might say, than you earn in a year.'

Sally said, in a voice like a gong, 'I think that's disgusting!'

Her eyes shone heroically; her head lifted proudly out of the collar of her moth-eaten jacket. She was young and indignant and beautiful.

George looked at her and felt weak with love. He said gently, 'Well, in a way . . .'

'Not *in a way*! Absolutely! Daddy does a useful job and gets paid for it. More than most people which isn't right, is it? You should be paid according to your needs not your talents, but that's not the point. I mean, to make money in this way is disgusting. It would take some people eight years to earn eight thousand pounds. It's not fair.'

Sam said, 'Life isn't fair, Sal.'

'Oh, don't be bloody stupid. You don't have to accept unfairness do you? And even if you're too feeble to make some real change in society, you don't have to buy another house when you've already got one to live in, when some people haven't a roof over their heads, when they're sleeping on park benches and in damp, dirty basements with rats crawling over their children's faces at night! That's not just unfair, either. It's criminally *wicked*!'

Sam said carefully, 'In principle I agree with you, Sally. But in practice, if I don't buy this cottage, or someone like me with money, to put it in order, it will fall down eventually. And if I do buy it, none of the people we're both concerned with will be affected one way or the other.'

'That's just the kind of awful, corrupt argument the capitalist system makes use of to keep itself going!'

Sam laughed. 'Keep myself going, more like. Digging a garden every day keeps the coronary away.'

'You could dig the garden and paint the house and then give it away to someone who needed it, couldn't you?'

'And if you'd stayed at home instead of swanning off to Switzerland this Christmas, you could have sent the money to starving Chinese,' Claire's father said. 'Don't talk such rubbish, Sally.'

'The Chinese aren't starving. They've got a *decent* system going. And it's not rubbish! *Dad* knows it isn't, he's been poor, but I suppose I couldn't expect you to know it! Dad's just a *tool*, a prisoner of the whole, degrading, horrible money thing, but it's people like you who make the prison. If Dad buys this place he'll be a traitor to his class but he

85

wouldn't ever have been if he hadn't married Mummy and you hadn't always made him feel poor and inferior. Talking about risk and margins and trust funds as if nothing else mattered, as if no one like Dad who did a proper job and got paid for it was of any importance at all. That's all you *do* talk about, except the awfulness of people who dare to get in your way, like strikers and tax-collectors and the one or two politicians who happen to believe there are more important things in life than your bank account! That sort of talk makes decent people feel sick, if you want to know. You make *me* feel sick.'

Sam said, 'Please don't talk to your grandfather like this, Sally.'

'I shall talk how I fucking well like. He *invited* it!'

'Sally!'

'I can take care of myself, thank you, Sam.' Claire's father's face was the ripe colour of an old brick wall with the sun shining on it, but his eyes were cold and amused. Like his daughter's, George saw. Claire was watching him and half-smiling. He said, amiably, 'You want your bottom smacked, Sally. Not for your childish opinions which don't interest anyone, but to teach you not to make a silly ass of yourself. You're not ten years old any longer.'

She gave a loud shriek of rage and launched herself at him, fists flying. He laughed and caught her wrists neatly, holding her at arm's length. He was a strong old man. She struggled, throwing herself forward and back and he released one hand and slapped her face hard. It looked to George as if he enjoyed doing this. She shouted, 'Damn you to hell,' and collapsed on the floor, helpless and moaning, knees drawn up to her chest, tugging her hair.

George left the room. Zeynep had removed herself earlier and was sitting on the stairs. She made way for George with a sullen look and he said, to ease what he supposed must be painful embarrassment, 'I expect families are much the same everywhere. Driving hell for leather across country Sunday afternoons, to quarrel with each other.' She said nothing; her blank face, uplifted to his, was pale as cream in the dim light of the stairway. He said, 'You know, you don't look as if you'd been ski-ing. You're white as a lily.'

But she didn't answer this either; simply hunched herself up, chin on her knees, hands holding her ankles, staring at nothing. In the room behind them, Sally was weeping.

George went into the garden. It was not yet quite dark but a fine, cold rain had begun to fall. He made his way round the back of the cottage, through a tangle of nettles and briars to what had, at one time, been an old-fashioned wash-house. There was an ancient copper in one corner and some rusted garden tools in another. Otherwise it was empty. It smelt of damp, decay, and something less pleasant; some sweet, rotting smell. A dead rat, perhaps, in the rafters? But at least it was shelter. Out of earshot of Sally's sad sobbing.

George turned up his collar and waited. Claire's father joined him, running round the corner of the house with surprising speed and grace; although big, he was muscular, kept his mountain of flesh under control. His emotions, too. He grinned cheerfully at George and said, 'What was all that about, d'you know? Can't think I deserved it.'

'No,' George said. 'I'm sorry.'

'Whipping-boy for something else, I daresay. Can't think what, though. She was all right at lunch. Sweet as sugar candy, tucking into the oysters paid for by this wicked capitalist without much sign of conscience. Oh well. Can't expect logic from women. Mind you, she's got spunk. Doesn't trim her sails – I like that. Not that you can let this sort of thing *pass*, doncher know, but I thought, best leave it to Sam to fire a few warning shots over her bows. No point in bringing up the big battleship!'

That suited him, George thought. A powerful old man, built like a battleship. How did Sam figure in this naval engagement? As an armed merchant cruiser?

Claire's father hopped lightly from one foot to the other. 'Bloody cold. Raw. Hope it doesn't take Sam too long to read the riot act.' He looked hopefully at George. 'Unless you've got your motor car here?'

'Sam drove me.'

'Pity. We're stuck then. I came with Claire. You know, they could turn this place into a sauna if Sam goes through with the deal, it's about the right size. You got a sauna, George?'

'No.'

'Finest thing out for toning you up, getting the poisons out.' He blew on his hands, then shook his head back. His hair was a bleached version of Claire's; a thick, healthy, silvery mane. He said, 'Chip off the old block, you know. Took me right back, hearing her rant on like that. I had much the same thing from Claire when she wanted to marry Sam. I wasn't keen for a number of reasons and she ripped into me – got her own way in the end, of course.' He stopped, remembering perhaps how she had in fact achieved this.

George said, 'It's turned out all right, hasn't it?' He felt numb; frozen internally.

'Oh, Sam's a good lad. Wish they'd managed a boy, though. I can say that to you, George. You won't mis-understand me. You build up an empire of sorts, you want someone to take over when you hand your chips in. What's it all for, otherwise?' He sighed gustily. 'I'm delighted with Sally, of course. But there are times when I'd give my right hand for a grandson,' He doubled his fist up and looked at it.

'I'm sorry,' George said.

He had a terrible desire to laugh. This vulgar, innocent old man! No, not laughter – that was no answer. What he wanted – *needed* – was the guts to give way to some more violent reaction; to smash, break, tear down. Rupture the delicate thread civilized life depended upon.

'Well, you can't have everything,' Claire's father said.

His daughter called out, 'There you are!' She approached them, stepping daintily as a deer. She had tied her scarf round her head; rain hung on her lashes like tears. 'All quiet now, thankfully. Sam's taking the girls. I'll drive you home, George, on the way back to London.'

'Is she all right?' her father asked. He emerged from the wash-house with a slight air of caution.

'More or less. Ashamed, anyway. I think it was probably a pre-menstrual thing, she does get tense sometimes. Hits out at the nearest thing. I'm sorry it was you, Pa. I expect she'll be sorry tomorrow.' She stood in front of them, smiling. 'What a place to hide!'

'I've hid in wash-houses before,' her father said. 'My grandmother's. She used to take in the neighbour's washing sometimes to earn a bit extra and I used to help mangle the sheets. Might tell Sally that! Establish my working-class origins!'

'She wouldn't believe you, Pa darling,' Claire said. 'And it's irrelevant, anyway. She was just grabbing a stick to beat someone with. It wasn't, really, what she was upset about.'

It seemed to George that she looked at him thoughtfully. With an air of complicity? But then he had often felt that and believed he imagined it. Claire wasn't sly. If she'd thought Sally had flown off the handle because he was marrying Leila, she would certainly say so. The thought that she might terrified him. He said, 'I can walk home. There's no need to take you out of your way.'

'In the rain?'

'I like rain.'

Claire looked at him quizzically.

Her father said, 'You two go on. I won't be a minute.'

George walked slowly away from the wash-house. This seemed to him like a conspiracy. To leave him alone with Claire so she could discuss Sally? How much did Claire know? Had Sally told her? He saw Sally in his mind's eye, lying on her bed, weeping, late at night, and her mother coming to comfort her. Stroking back the streaked, silver-blonde hair and saying, 'What is it, my lamb?'

Claire jabbed her elbow into his side and hissed, 'He wants to *pee*, you old fool.'

They waited for him at the gate. George thought that Claire was waiting for him to speak. In the rain, the cottage looked desolate. He thought – next week I shall be in Istanbul. Mosques, minarets, beggars. Of course, at this time of the year, it rained in Istanbul, too. The weather was always uncertain there, as he was careful to point out in his travel brochures. There is this great bond between the Turks and the English: they both enjoy discussing the weather because they are never sure what it will do. He said, 'Do you think Sam will buy it?'

'The cottage? God knows.'

She sighed. Her expression was distant as if her thoughts were turned inward. Wondering how to bring up a difficult subject?

He said nervously, 'Funny girl, Zeynep.'

'Oh, she despises us all.'

'But Sally gets on with her?'

'Yes.'

'That's the main thing.'

'Sally looks up to her. She says Zeynep is a serious person. She admires that.'

'So Sam said. Does Zeynep ever talk?'

'Sometimes. She occasionally says things like, *it is our duty to soak the blood from the rich*!' She looked at him levelly and his stomach shrank. She said, 'George, will you really be happy?'

He couldn't think what she was talking about. He was thinking of Sally. Waiting for Claire to accuse him. She narrowed her nose in the way that sometimes made her look crafty and said, 'With Leila, of course.'

'Oh. Yes. I hope so.'

'I wasn't very nice that time you took us out to dinner. Sam pointed it out afterwards.'

'You were moderately bitchy. I don't think she noticed. Even if she had done, she wouldn't have been surprised, or held it against you. She doesn't expect people to like her. She doesn't have many expectations at all.'

'I'm sorry. I'm sorry that I behaved badly.' Claire rarely apologized. Having got this off her chest she smiled with relief, as if she had accomplished some enormously difficult task. There had been nothing else troubling her.

They rounded the bend in the narrow lane, Claire driving, as always, too fast, and almost ran into the back of Sam's car. The bonnet was up and he was peering into the engine. George got out. Sam said, 'Carburettor, I think. Bloody awkward place to stop. Sorry.'

Sally was holding the flash-lamp. Wet hair hid her face. Her hand trembled.

Sam said, 'Hold it steady, can't you?'

Her voice trembled, too. 'I'm sorry, Daddy.'

George's presence was making things worse for her. He said, to Sam, 'Can you fix it?'

'I think so. Ask Claire to hang on a minute in case I can't, will you?'

It was raining hard now. Claire said, 'Tell that silly girl, Zeynep, to get back in the car. No point in her getting soaked, too.'

91

Zeynep had walked a little way down the lane, to a gateway, She stood, foot on the bottom rung, staring into into the dark, empty field.

George said, 'You'll get wet.'

She shook her head scornfully. For some mad reason she had put on dark glasses. Hiding behind them? They made her look blind.

George felt foolish in this nanny's role. He said, 'Claire's worried about you.'

He turned away and she said, 'Mr Hare, I must ask you something . . .'

A low, hurried voice. At least she could speak! Perhaps she really was only shy; that contemptuous manner a defence, like the glasses.

Rain ran down his neck. He turned up his coat collar.

She said, 'It is not very important. Just that you guessed rightly. I did not go ski-ing with Sally. Or not all the time.'

She hesitated. He thought – I'm not going to help her!

She seemed to be looking at the back of Claire's car. Not that he could tell, really. He said, softening, 'It's all right. We're well out of earshot.'

'I would not want to upset Mr and Mrs Catto. They have been kind to me.'

'They wouldn't like to think Sally had been ski-ing alone? Or they'd tell your parents?'

'Both. I am afraid of both things. Sally was all right. There were other girls at the hotel she made friends with. And I had to see a friend in Berlin. My parents don't like him.'

So Sally played gooseberry? Well, she was old enough to look after herself. On the pill anyway, he thought grimly. And this spoilt girl's love affairs were not his concern. Could she really be worried Claire would give her away? Perhaps. She had the free, passionate manner of a wealthy

American girl but she was still Turkish in origin. *Lock up your daughters* . . .

She had taken off her glasses. It was too dark, now, to see her face, but the gesture disarmed him. She said, 'Please . . .' in a soft, cozening voice and he felt a faint, sexual flutter.

He said, 'Don't worry. I won't say anything. Why should I? It's none of my business.'

Chapter 5

A letter from Sally.

Dear George,

I must apologize for my abysmal behaviour. I felt that my life had come to an end but I see now it was only a turning point. Everything is changed for me now. When I leave school I shall take a social science diploma and try to look after those less fortunate than myself. I would like to change the world but since that is not possible I shall probably look after handicapped children. This is not a pathetic adolescent whim but a real change of direction. There are compensations in the saddest lives and I shall try to make the best use of mine.

I hope you and Leila will have a long and happy marriage.

Peace and love!

Sally.

George carried this letter with him for over a year: to his wedding, to his grandmother's funeral, to board-meetings, to parties, to every occasion happy or sad or neither one nor the other at which he was present during that time, until his wallet was stolen out of his back trouser pocket, while he was having his shoes cleaned outside the Büyük Efes Hotel in Izmir. Since he paid the shoe cleaner with loose change he did not know he had lost his wallet until an hour or so later when he was lunching with his old friend, Omer, at a café beside the great bay. Omer had flown in that morning to discuss a scheme George had proposed for building a holiday village sixty miles from Izmir. It was early in June and exceptionally hot. A breeze from the sea brought the sweet smell of sewage, for which Izmir is famous, and billowed the canvas canopy beneath which they sat, eating lobsters. George listening; Omer talking.

He was telling George a story about one of the unit trust companies he had established two years ago. It had been so successful that one of the big banks had persuaded – or bribed – a newspaper to publish an article suggesting that the trust was unsound. Hundreds of small investors had withdrawn their capital and the company had collapsed. Omer had taken legal action; the case had dragged on for two years until last week when the judge ruled that the article was libellous and ordered a public retraction. But on the day this was to be published it had been pushed off the front page by the story of a hi-jacked plane, forced to land in Beirut.

Omer punctuated his account of this misfortune with little, unwilling trills of laughter, dabbing the corners of his eyes with his napkin. The ironic joke was, his own brother had been on the hi-jacked plane! He had been freed after two days and claimed to have been well treated within the limits of certain unavoidable discomforts; had even praised the considerate behaviour of the young men who were holding him prisoner, in a temperature of a hundred and four degrees fahrenheit, and threatening to kill him. There had been a six-year-old boy among the passengers and the hi-jackers had made a pet of him, giving him sweets and letting him play in the cockpit where the smell from the blocked lavatories was less offensive. Eventually, they had offered to let the child leave with his mother but she had refused to go, bravely insisting that his presence might safeguard the lives of the others. 'She may have been right.' Omer said. 'Those lads aren't vicious. Most of them are just wayward children.'

'Oh, for God's sake, Omer! Suppose they had blown up the plane!'

'Then I'd call them terrorists, naturally.' Omer laughed merrily, mopping his eyes. 'But one must never argue from hypotheses, my old friend. It blunts the judgement.'

George supposed Omer must be temporarily unhinged with relief because his brother was alive and not scattered in pieces all over the airfield. 'They were threatening to kill a plane-load of innocent people. That's not an hypothesis. Coercive intimidation is the definition of terrorism, surely?'

'It's a word we use too easily.' Omer was all at once emphatically serious; unsmiling, his plump face looked naked and sad and very much older. 'We use it in fear. To reassure ourselves that society is quite satisfactory, only needs a bit of tinkering with here and there, and that any group that wants radical change is necessarily criminal. You don't dare speak the truth, which is that life is ugly and that some romantic young people are impatient to change it, because that would undermine your complacency. So you go red in the face and shout *terrorist*! Not you, personally, my friend.'

'Thank you.' George, who had been feeling in his back pocket, realized now that his wallet had gone. He was trying to remember how much money had been in it. He said, 'I agree with you about the emotive misuse of language. Or would you say that to call a hi-jacker a romantic young man was simply to take a different point of view? I didn't think you were a revolutionary, Omer.'

'I have friends who have children who are. In varying

96

degrees, of course. As I expect you, in England, have friends whose children join protest marches and organize sit-ins at their universities.'

'Not quite the same thing.'

'You know that the situation is different. Students who take part in the sort of activities you would regard fairly indulgently are treated severely here. Some of them are in prison for owning an edition of Marx. Children I have bounced on my knee!'

George thought of Sally quoting Mao. She was coming to Turkey; was perhaps already here. When George had left England, three weeks before, final arrangements had not yet been made. He thought – I must ask Omer.

He had lost Sally's letter. It had been tucked into the zipped section of his wallet along with a ten-dollar bill for emergencies, a cautious habit his grandmother had taught him, sending him off to school with a two-shilling bit in the inner flap of his blazer's breast pocket. 'Have you got your handkerchief, George? And your emergency money?'

He thought of his grandmother, standing at the garden gate and waving goodbye to him. He thought of his safe, cushioned life. He said, 'I can see that might make one's attitude a bit ambivalent. Though not towards hi-jackers, surely?'

'They are children too,' Omer said.

George said to Leila, 'I've had my wallet pinched.' She lay on the bed in the air-conditioned hotel room with damp, cotton wool pads on her eyes. When George spoke she moaned softly in answer; a faint, exhausted sound, like someone dying at the bottom of a pit.

George said, 'Not that it matters. The insurance will cover it. Bloody bore about the credit cards, though. Are you feeling better?'

She took the pads from her eyes and blinked at him wanly.

He said, 'Omer sends you his love. He was sorry you weren't at lunch. He says he hopes you'll be better tomorrow when we drive out to look at the site.'

'I hope I'll be up to it. The heat is so terrible, George! I didn't realize it would be so much worse than Istanbul. And although the air-conditioning cools the room down it makes me feel clammy. I did open the window for a while but the noise from the swimming pool was so ghastly I had to close it again.'

He sat on the end of the bed and put his hand gently on the soles of her pretty, bare feet. 'Tummy better?'

She said, reluctantly, 'A little, perhaps. The cramps have eased up. I never know which is worse, to be loose and apprehensive or totally gummed up so that your inside feels like concrete. I don't know if I've got a bug or if it's my nerves. Whatever it is, it makes travelling an absolute nightmare.'

He stroked her feet rhythmically. This sometimes soothed her. 'My poor darling.'

'I do hope I'm not developing a spastic colon.'

'I hope not, too.' he said, with feeling. And then, to distract her from the state of her bowels, 'Omer's brother was on that hi-jacked plane. His older brother, the one he's staying with, in Izmir. He's safe now, thankfully, but it must have been a fearful couple of days for the family.'

Leila said, 'Those dreadful young thugs!'

'It's not quite as simple as that.' He knew it would be wiser to leave it there. But he said, 'In Turkey, the line between idealist and thug is a hard one to draw.'

'Not for me it isn't.'

Her triumphant look irritated him. 'Even for you it might be. If you'd *listen*!'

She sighed with exaggerated patience. 'I'm afraid I'm against violence. So spare me your cleverness, George.

I know you can argue black's white but even if I'm not very intellectual, I know my own mind, and nothing you can tell me can change it. And I'm really not well enough for a pointless discussion, I'd have thought you'd see that.'

She closed her eyes. George sat silent in front of this barrier. It depressed him that she should elevate lack of interest into a virtue even though he thought he knew why she did it. She had needed for so long to come first with someone that anything that seemed to remove him from her, however briefly, made her frightened and angry.

They had spent an evening in Istanbul with old friends of his. Arthur Bone was at the British Consulate; a large, plain, kind man with a large, plain, kind wife. They were first cousins and could have been taken for twins they looked so alike, both with long, heavy limbs and mild-eyed, equine faces – rather like a pair of gentle dray horses, George sometimes thought. Even their voices were similar: sexlessly high-pitched, upper-class, slightly whinnying.

They were middle-aged, childless, and enthusiastically enquiring. Any ignorance on their part was a challenge to be seized with delight as a splendid chance to learn something new. They overwhelmed Leila with their size, their kind smiles, their innocent interest. They asked her about herself, her likes and dislikes, what she knew and what she thought about Turkey, and when she said she knew nothing they hurried to inform her as they would have wished to be informed in her place. Leila saw their questions as impertinence, their fulsome explanations as condescension. She answered shortly, tight-lipped and flushed. They thought this reaction was shyness and continued their educative efforts on a less personal plane, speaking in a kind of harmonious duet about Atatürk, the key role of the Army in Turkish politics, and the recent outbreak of urban terrorism

99

that had led to martial law being imposed. 'But you must understand, Leila,' Arthur Bone said, 'that the situation here is quite different from the situation in Greece. There you have a simple, old-fashioned, military dictatorship. In Turkey, the Army see themselves, not as oppressors, but as the guardians of Atatürk's ideal European state.'

'Rightly to some extent, dear,' Mary murmured.

Arthur nodded. 'Yes, of course. They didn't oppose the introduction of democratic forms in 1945, for example. And they haven't overthrown the Turkish Parliament now. They simply stepped in when it had, in effect, ceased to govern.'

'I'm afraid I don't understand politics,' Leila said.

When the meal was over, Mary Bone went to the kitchen and came back with the coffee-tray, looking anxious. The young maid had locked herself in her bedroom. She said, apologetically, 'I'm sorry, but it is rather worrying. She is very ignorant, you see, a girl from the country, and we're afraid she may be in trouble. There are students in the house opposite.' She looked at her husband. 'Are they there now, dear?'

On one side the large room they sat in looked over the Golden Horn; on the other, a narrow street. Arthur switched off the lights and George joined him at this window. At another darkened window, on the ground floor of an apartment house opposite, a cigarette glowed, disappeared, glowed again.

Mary said regretfully, 'I'm afraid it must be a signal, Arthur.'

He drew the curtains and switched the lights on again. He said, 'Pour the coffee, dear.'

Mary said, 'Of course, it may only be a love affair.'

'I think it would be prudent to doubt it.' Arthur beamed kindly at Leila, suddenly seeing, perhaps, a practical way of enlightening her on a subject she seemed to find difficult.

'One has to steer a sensible course between foolish complacency and fearing there may be anarchists beneath every bed. The boy – or boys – over there may be perfectly innocent. But if they do belong to one of the student extremist groups, Dev Genc, say, or the People's Liberation Army, it is quite possible that they are using our poor little maid to keep an eye on the house.'

Mary said, 'Do you like Turkish or French coffee, Leila? Or would you prefer Sanka? I find that it suits me better at night.' As she passed the cups, her large, fair hand shook a little.

Arthur said, 'The tragedy is, of course, that these young men are being used, too. By Russian agents working through East Berlin, and by Syria and Bulgaria and Iraq, to damage the Nato defence structure as well as the fabric of society. It has become an intelligence operation manipulated from the outside instead of an internal revolutionary movement. There is a wild streak of destructive romanticism, almost a death-wish, in some Turkish young people. It makes them easy tools for evil men.'

'That's unlike you, Arthur,' Mary said. 'To use the word evil about any man.'

Her mild eyes reproached him. He put his cup down on the low table between them and reached across it to touch her wrist lightly. 'I was upset,' he said. 'I hate to see you frightened.' He smiled proudly at Leila and George. 'It's a rare thing, I promise you. Mary is the bravest woman I know.'

Leila said, 'Why is she afraid now?'

Arthur gave his shy, whinnying laugh. 'Not for herself, of course, but for me. She's afraid I'll be kidnapped and murdered like the Israeli consul. Though it's not really likely. Any diplomat is fair game, but I'm very small beer. Not a valuable hostage! Mary knows it, too. It's only this silly business with our maid that has made her so nervous.'

He smiled lovingly at his wife. 'Perhaps you're right, dear. It may be nothing more than a young love affair, after all. They stand at their windows and watch for each other . . .'

Mary said, 'She could let them in any time. Any time, Arthur!'

Leila was looking amazed. 'If you believe that, why don't you ring up the police and tell them?'

'This isn't England, darling,' George said.

Arthur Bone explained, very gently, that if they were to inform the police, the girl would be taken in for questioning and, quite probably, tortured.

Mary shuddered. 'One hears such terrible stories. Of course, we could send the child home to her village. But I can't bear to do it. She has had such a tragic life. Her mother was killed in an earthquake and her father is very reactionary. An old-style Moslem with the traditional attitudes towards women. She has never been allowed to go to school, even!'

'Mary is teaching her to read and write,' Arthur said. 'She is learning quite fast, isn't she, dear? She's not a clever girl, but Mary is a wonderful teacher.'

'I am patient, that's all,' Mary said. 'But you do see, don't you, that we can't just send her away? Certainly not on such flimsy evidence. It's the only chance she has, to live here with us, and learn to read.'

'That's all very well, isn't it?' Leila tossed her head angrily and spoke as if she felt some personal grievance. As perhaps she did, George thought. Their kindly forbearance was an insult to her, a clever way of suggesting that she lacked their informed understanding! 'You'll feel differently, Mary, if your husband is murdered because of her, won't you?'

Lying on her bed in the Büyük Efes Hotel in Izmir, Leila opened her eyes. George was standing at the window and looking out over the darkening bay. He wondered if Leila could be coaxed to leave the hotel and walk by the water. Perhaps, tomorrow, she would feel well enough to drive out to the site for the holiday village. The inspection of the site would not interest her much, but she could spend the day on the terrace of the small hotel there, where the food was carefully adapted to the hygienic taste of the Americans from the Nato base at Izmir, and in the cool of the evening, he would take her to the Temple of Apollo at Claros. She found ruins boring, but the guardian was a friend of his, an old Turk from Salonika, and the road to it was beautiful; winding between gentle, green hills and lively with small farms and people and chickens and goats. The last time he had gone there he had seen three coal-black baby donkeys trotting in single file along the ridge of a hill . . .

He longed for her to love this country as he did. If only she would raise her eyes from the dirt and the flies.

Leila said, 'Suppose Sally had been on that hi-jacked plane. You'd feel differently about terrorists then, wouldn't you?'

She didn't know how he felt about Sally. Sally was the beloved child of his best friends. Sam and Claire were carefully kind to Leila and Sally was elaborately polite. In Leila's presence, she took refuge in an artificial childhood; often wearing school uniform and long, white socks, and speaking about the grinding bore of Latin homework and her A-level examinations which she intended to take a term early. The last time they had seen her she had been full of the holiday she was going to spend with Omer and his wife, and with Zeynep, who was already in Turkey. She said, 'It'll be simply *fabulous*, Leila, if you and Uncle George are in Istanbul at the same time!' George was astonished by the ease and consistency with which she played this unnatural role. Leila said, 'She's a bit young for her age, isn't she?

And, of course, ridiculously spoiled!' No one had ever spoiled *her!* She said, 'I must say, I'm glad I haven't got a daughter that age.'

Leila had miscarried six months after they married. She had a terrible time in the hospital. The foetus had been removed manually and without anaesthetic by a sadistic Armenian registrar. Afterwards, he sat on Leila's bed and stroked her arms and told her that women got sexual enjoyment from pain. He was a madman as well as a sadist. He said that if it had not been for the Turks, who had murdered most of his nation, the Armenians would have been the masters of Europe.

Repeating this to George, Leila had spoken so calmly that he thought at first she must have imagined, or at least embroidered, the incident. But the truth was more subtle. Leila had always seen herself as a victim and now she was vindicated. She would have complained more had the outrage been less. As it was, she could afford to be generous. She agreed that George should tell the consultant gynaecologist about his registrar's behaviour but only so that other women should not suffer. 'I don't want to make trouble for the poor man on *my* account. I daresay he's had enough in his time or he would never have treated me like that. People are only cruel when they've been hurt too often themselves.'

She smiled at George sadly. He understood the inference he was expected to draw and regretted that Leila should find it necessary to improve even this shining hour, but he was touched, none the less. As he kissed her, it struck him as a pity that she should only show herself at her best in adversity. Then he dismissed this thought, like an unwelcome visitor, and resolved, as far as he could, to see she was not hurt again.

He was beginning to realize how hard a task this was likely to be. She had such a sharp eye for slights, such deep wells of resentment, such energy in her anger. She had lain on her bed with closed eyes for over an hour now, pretending to doze but in fact brooding darkly over that one sentence of his. He knew which one, exactly . . .

He said, 'If anyone I knew had been on that plane, I'd have been distraught, naturally. It's not an argument.'

'You always twist and turn, George. Never give a straight answer! I said *Sally*. Not *anyone*!'

'I might have been marginally more distraught, then. It's a convention that one worries more about the young. A stupid one, possibly, because they're often less vulnerable. They know less and so they're less easily frightened. But of course if she'd been in that kind of danger I'd have been out of my mind. You know that I love the child.' It gave him exquisite pleasure to have a chance to say this. He sat on the bed and took Leila's hand. Partly in gratitude, partly in penance. He said, 'This is such a silly game, darling.'

'Not to me. I've been lying here, trying to see your point of view. I can't, as it happens, but that's not what upsets me. What does, is that you never try to see mine. I really don't think you do, George. You're so sure of yourself. All you ever say is, *if only you'd listen*!'

'I think I said, if you'd listen. Not, if *only*.'

But he couldn't be sure. She was probably right; she had a mind like a tape recorder. And the effect was the same, anyway.

She was shaking her head and sighing.

He said, 'I'm sorry, darling.'

'That's easy to say, isn't it? I'm sorry, I'm sorry! I sometimes think you'd make a good Catholic, George! Behave as you please – as long as you make a good act of contrition!'

'I don't think good Catholics really think that.'

'Roland did. He used to cross himself before he went out and then get into the car and drive like a fiend! Oh – that was just comic, but other things weren't, you know! He'd get drunk and bash me up and then trot down to confession and come back feeling virtuous! Clean as a new born lamb! That *sickened* me, George!'

Her large eyes watched him, full of pain. Even if it was self-inflicted, it was still pain.

He said, 'My poor love. But you know you really are looking much better. Rested. And your eyes are beautifully clear. Would you like to go out and look at the bay? It's much cooler now, even if it still stinks a bit. We could walk or take a horse carriage, whatever you like. Perhaps eat a bit later, if you feel up to it.'

'I think I could manage something light. Somewhere clean.'

'We'll find somewhere clean.'

She smiled at him reluctantly. He took her hands and pulled her up off the bed and held her against him for a minute, then let her go to the bathroom. He waited while she showered, listening to the sound of the water, sitting by the window and cracking his knuckle joints. She came back into the room, wrapped in a white towel, and said '*George!*'

Her voice was desperate. He leapt up as if shot.

'George! Roland wasn't a Catholic.'

He looked at her despairing face and controlled his laughter. 'I must say, it did cross my mind. Odd that you'd not mentioned it before!'

'I don't know why I say these things!'

'You were trying to say something about the slippery ease with which I apologize.'

'I suppose so.'

'Although I did mean it. I was sorry.'

'I knew you were. That's the terrible thing.'

He crossed the room and put his arms round her. She was trembling. She smelt damp and clean and warm. He said, 'A little dramatic exaggeration isn't a crime.'

'There was a kind of truth in it. He'd knock me about and then go to the pub and have a maudlin conversation with some man or other about how ghastly women were and how a bit of the rough stuff was the only way to treat them. Then he'd come back and say he hoped I felt better now and where was his supper?'

'Poor love.'

'Don't be sorry for me. I don't deserve it. Oh – I despise myself sometimes. The way I try to get a moral advantage out of my unhappy life.'

'Most people do that, one way or another.'

'You don't.'

'I've not been unhappy.'

'So you always say. I even resent that sometimes. Why should *you* have escaped? It's not *fair* . . .'

George laughed.

She said, 'I wish I was different.'

'I like you as you are.'

This was true. Or he had decided to make it true. He kissed her and she sighed, pleasurably. She found confession as relaxing as orgasm. 'I'm sorry if I was stupid about Sally. I'm simply jealous of anyone else that you love. And I suppose I feel guilty because our baby died.'

'That was hardly your fault.'

'If I'd been younger and stronger I'd have tried again. Even if I had been just a bit braver. But I couldn't face it again. I really couldn't, George.'

'I don't want you to. I don't want children. I'm too old and too selfish. I only want you to be happy and well.'

'If I could believe that, I would be.'

This was the obvious answer and she made it automatically, but it seemed to him that for once she had spoken the desolate truth.

He said, saddened, 'You must trust me, then,' knowing

that she never would, that she couldn't, it was not in her nature, and that she was right not to, because although he believed he would continue to behave as if he were trust-worthy, it would be a matter of effort and discipline and even if that added up, practically, to the same thing in the end, it was not the same thing in fact. And in some deep, hidden part of herself, she probably knew it.

Leila was a child, really. Younger, in some ways, than Sally. Had retained, into middle life, a child's innocent belief that if you wailed loud enough, kicked and screamed and protested, some miraculous agency would put the world right.

Sally knew that wasn't true. That letter he had kept for so long, and lost now, had an adult dignity in its deliberate childishness. She had written to him as if she were still only a child, to comfort him.

And he had been comforted. He had read and re-read her letter, and smiled. It made him feel about ninety years old.

Sally was in Istanbul now. Her plane had not crashed, nor been hi-jacked. She was a lucky, privileged girl, sent by her rich parents to stay with a Turkish friend for the summer.

Omer had a house in Ankara, a flat in Istanbul, and a villa on an island in the Sea of Marmara. Like most rich Turks, he moved out of the city in the summer. To get to his island, they had to catch a boat very early in the morning. George said to Leila, 'Do you want to go, darling? It'll be a bit of a scrum.'

He longed to see Sally, and dreaded it. He was as jumpy as a boy.

'Why not?' Leila said.

This fine, Sunday morning in Istanbul was one of her good days. It was hot, but not as hot as Izmir. She had slept well, her bowels were in order, her hair newly washed.

She said, 'Why are you being so difficult, George? Don't you want to see Sally?'

The Galata Bridge landing-stage was crowded with families, jostling and shouting, setting off for a day on the islands. They fought to buy tickets and, as soon as the gangway was down, surged off the pontoon and onto the boat like water through a breach in a dam. George had his arm round Leila, protecting her. She was flushed and excited and laughing. They pushed their way to the upper deck and found canvas seats by the rail. People were playing cards, feeding children, drinking warm, bottled fruit-juices and watered yoghurt, buying biscuits made with sesame seeds. Empty bottles and cardboard cartons and fruit parings bobbed in the creamy wake of the boat. 'It's like one vast picnic,' Leila said. She tied a scarf round her head and lifted her face to the wind. George touched her cheek tenderly. Her happiness was fragile as glass; a light blow would break it. He said, 'Oh, the Turks are great people for picnics.'

At Prince's Island, they got off to wait for a smaller boat. Men were fishing from the jetty. The gravelly beach was grey, covered with crumpled newspapers and dead jellyfish. Beneath a banner proclaiming that the orders of the military government must be obeyed, tourist carriages waited, drawn by skeleton-thin horses, hung with coloured harness and bells.

The small boat was almost empty. Omer's island was its first call; a smooth hump, like the back of a green whale, lifting out of the water.

They walked up a dusty road, noisy with crickets, past several new houses. 'Those weren't here when I came last year,' George said. 'Omer must be selling off land.'

He felt a faint disappointment. He had remembered the island as a secluded, romantic place; had been sentimentally pleased to picture Sally there. A young girl in a floppy hat, dreaming.

Omer was waiting for them at the gate of his villa, an old, wooden house with lacey balconies and elaborately carved shutters from which the paint had peeled long ago. 'It reminds me of Russia,' Leila said. 'Although of course I have never been there.'

Omer smiled. He wore a bright yellow shirt and white swimming trunks. His strong, hairy legs glistened, as if he had only just emerged from the sea. He said, in a soft, amused voice, 'The border with that country is unfortunately close, so the architecture is somewhat similar.'

They were to swim before lunch. Omer led the way to the shore, down through the overgrown, tangled garden. George held Leila's hand although it would have been easier to negotiate the narrow path single file. He had taken it instinctively but as they descended he realized why he continued to hold it. He wanted to appear before Sally hand in hand with his wife.

But she was not there to observe this protective display of marital felicity. Only Omer's wife, Nili, was waiting to greet them. She was sunbathing on a small, concrete platform, jutting out into the sea. A slender, very young woman with a well-tended air, shyly smiling. As George kissed her cheek and introduced Leila, his eyes flickered past her. She said, 'Sally's swimming.'

He could see her blonde head far out in the water. He shaded his eyes with his hand and said heartily, 'There she blows.'

Omer said, 'I thought she was afraid of the jelly-fish. I am afraid we have a great many this morning.'

They were clustered thickly round the iron steps at the side of the platform; pale, floating circles of almost transparent flesh, twitching with unseen, delicate muscles.

Omer said, 'It really is unusual to see so many. But you need not be frightened. They are not a dangerous variety.'

Leila shivered. 'Horrible, though!'

'They come and go with the wind. Perhaps the wind will change later.' Omer looked saddened. He was the kind of host who makes plans, and the pre-lunch swim was part of his programme. He said, hopefully, 'They are only a little unpleasant until you get used to them.'

Nili smiled at Leila's shocked face. 'Don't let him bully you! I, too, will not swim with the jelly-fish. I am not brave, like Sally!'

The two women went up to the house. George changed into his trunks and sat with Omer, baking in the sun and watching Sally, who was swimming backwards and forwards, keeping a parallel line with the shore. Her hair streamed behind her. She was too far away for George to see her face. He thought she looked lonely.

He said, 'Where's Zeynep? I thought she'd be here, with Sally.'

Omer groaned. He lay on a striped mattress, blinking up at the white sun and groaning. He said, 'Oh, that girl!'

'What's happened to her?'

'She's at the flat in 'Stanbul.' Omer rolled on his side and propped himself upon his elbow. 'She's been here since October.'

'At the university?'

'Yes. She stayed with an old aunt of her mother's until a couple of months ago. Then the aunt got ill and she came to us. But she refused to move out to the villa when we did and that has created something of a domestic storm, I'm afraid. It really is most unsuitable that a young woman should stay alone in the city! But she was very determined to do so and her parents seemed content that she should. Nili telephoned them, naturally. They said she was old enough to make up her own mind.'

George remembered that cool, intransigent stare. 'I'd guess she was used to looking after herself.'

Omer said, disapprovingly, 'Of course, she has been brought up in America. A girl on her own is regarded quite differently here. Nili is very shocked. She says no one will marry her now.'

George smiled.

'That seems foolish to you, I suppose.'

'Not at all.'

'I think Sally found it a strange attitude. It was unfortunate that this happened almost as soon as she got here. She had expected to spend some time with Zeynep.'

It seemed hard on Sally. George said, idly, 'She still could, couldn't she? They'd be all right, two girls together. I don't think Sam and Claire would be worried about Sally's marriage prospects.'

'Perhaps not. There are other dangers.'

George looked at Omer. His old friend lay on his side, plump chin sunk on plump chest, frowning out to sea. He thought – Omer's wife is not much older than Sally! He said, 'What, particularly?'

Omer shook his head. 'Nothing specific. Zeynep makes me uneasy.'

'I can understand that. I met her – oh, about sixteen months ago. In England. She had been ski-ing with Sally.' Only she hadn't been ski-ing. He thought of Mary Bone's little maid. He said, 'What are her friends like?'

'Other students, I imagine. I've not met them. She came and went as she pleased. Her parents made it clear we were not to feel responsible for her. She's not exactly communicative.'

'No,' George hesitated. 'I suppose she couldn't be mixed

up in something? Some student trouble?' He laughed, to show he thought this was, most probably, a ridiculous suggestion.

Omer said, 'She's very innocent politically. That could be dangerous in theory, I know, but in practice, who's likely to bother with her? In effect, she's an American girl. Not remotely interested in Turkish problems.' He sighed and scratched his stomach. 'At least, I've seen no sign of it.'

George dived off the iron steps. Opening his eyes under water, he looked up and saw the jelly-fish, massed solid above him. He surfaced and they bumped against his arm like smooth, slimy footballs. One slithered across his shoulders and down his back.

Further out, they grew fewer in number, but larger. Sally was treading water. Her silvery hair streamed around her like seaweed. He called to her and she swam towards him, face set and desperate.

He said, 'Beastly, aren't they?'

She nodded.

'But you'd rather face them than me, is that it?'

'Something like that.' She grinned at him. 'When Omer said you were coming, I felt sick. But it's all right now you're here.'

'Silly.' He felt extraordinarily happy. Out here, in the sea, they were just two people swimming. There were no complications. They could swim on for ever. He said, 'I'm afraid lunch is ready.'

A jelly-fish bumped her chin. She gave a little moan of aversion and closed her eyes.

He said, 'They won't hurt you. Omer says they don't sting. I suppose he must know.'

She shuddered and beat at the water.

'Swim close to me.' They were already close. Her warm,

frantic arms brushed against his. He put his arm round her waist. 'Is that better?'

She smiled at him so sweetly he felt as if he were dissolving with joy. 'Close your eyes and hold on to my shoulders. Swim on my back. I'll try and push them out of your way.'

It was all he could do for her. A small labour of love.

She clung to him until they reached the iron steps. Omer was standing there to take her hand and she went up in front of George, brown legs sluicing water on to his upturned face. As he followed her he had a sense of loss so acute it made him tremble. A moment ago she had been close to him, her breasts against his naked back, swimming as if they were part of each other. Now the land divided them; she stood apart, separate and untouchable.

She watched him as he hauled himself on to the landing-stage, holding herself very erect as if inviting him to look at her. Or challenging him, perhaps. Her shoulders were thrown back and her head lifted high.

Omer was saying something. Watching Sally, George heard only the end of the sentence. '. . . earthquake weather.'

He thought, for no reason it seemed, of Sam's mother. No – not for no reason: the involuntary associations of the mind were always logical. Earthquakes reminded him of his grandmother who was sensitive to barometric pressure. He had gone with her, one still, hot, summer evening to hear Sam's mother sing *The Messiah* in the Methodist Church choir; had sat, on hard seats in the hall, while she stood above them on the platform, belting out the Hallelujah Chorus. She had seemed magnificent to George, a beautiful woman like a dark queen, her head held high and her proud, full voice riding the storm of the music, and he had been furious with his grandmother when she gasped and turned pale and said she was sorry but she couldn't bear to stay any longer. She could feel thunder in the air.

Omer said, 'That was the last time we had so many jelly-fish. I remember now – I had been swimming at the weekend and two or three days later, I was on the boat going to Yalova. The wind had dropped, it was very still, and as we came close to the shore I saw a minaret move. Flick, flick, like an upside-down pendulum, through an angle of almost thirty degrees. It was an amazing sight.'

'Are we going to have an earthquake now?' Sally said. She had made an effort to keep the childish enthusiasm out of her voice, but her eyes were alight with it.

Omer shrugged. 'Perhaps a small one. Perhaps only a storm. Perhaps nothing – that there were jelly-fish, and then, three days later, an earthquake, may have been only a coincidence.'

'Don't you *know*?' Sally asked.

'I am not a geologist.'

'I know *that*,' she said. 'I meant, if you lived in a country where that sort of thing was likely to happen, you'd think you'd know what the signs were!'

'What would the point be? Most earthquakes are little ones, small tremors only – a heavy lorry passing the house would make more disturbance. In a bad earthquake you would be best out of doors, or in an old *hamam*. A bath-house. They withstand stress because of their structure. They are built with rounded roofs, like a beehive. But it would hardly be practicable to take refuge in one each time you saw a jelly-fish, say. And most other indications are equally dubious.'

George laughed. 'The real thing is, you'd rather not know what they were. Isn't that it?'

'Perhaps. I'm a fatalistic oriental, at heart.'

'Or an indefatigably lazy man?'

'I like to guard my peace,' Omer said.

Chapter 6

On his first visit to Istanbul, years ago now, George had been caught up in a brawl from which he had been lucky to emerge alive. This was his introduction to that dangerous, sprawling, golden ant-heap of a city. It was also the first time he met Arthur Bone.

George was attending a conference arranged by an organization called International Youth Travel. The British Consulate gave a party on the second night of the conference and Arthur was host. He said, to George, 'If you really want to know about Turkey, you should talk to the I.Y.T.'s representative here, Nejat Bey.' He took George into the circle round Nejat and moved on: his function, on this occasion, was to introduce people, not to warn them against each other.

Nejat Bey was a large, grizzled, young-old man with an expansive manner and a mouth full of gold teeth. George had observed him earlier, pacing the room like an imperious bear with a retinue of girls trailing after him. He gazed meltingly into George's eyes, flung a heavy arm round his shoulders, and said, 'Greetings, dear friend. Welcome to my beautiful country.' His hot, tobacco-scented breath fanned George's cheek.

George, twenty-five then, found Nejat exotic and formidable. But he was eager to learn about Turkey and since the party was almost over – the Consulate's supply of warm, watered whisky appeared to have finished – he gathered his courage and invited Nejat to lunch the next day.

'Tomorrow?' Nejat said. 'Tomorrow?' He flung back his head, displaying his mouth's shining treasure in a titanic shout of laughter. His thick fingers massaged the back of George's head, rumpling his hair. 'Tomorrow may never come, Mr Hare. We will dine together tonight. You and I, and a small, select group of good friends. We will have a wonderful time and get to know each other.'

They went to a restaurant on the Bosphorus, travelling in taxis and in the I.Y.T. minibus, driven by Nejat. They sat at a long table, Nejat at the head and George halfway down. Of the thirty people or so in this small, select group, he thought he only recognized two, a pale Dane with one arm who sat opposite him and the pretty Japanese girl on Nejat's right hand, but he was delighted to be here, grateful to Nejat for including him in his happy party. Raki was brought and they all toasted each other. Nejat said, 'I think, my dear friends, we will have lobster for all.' The waiter offered the wine list. Nejat waved it away with one huge, hairy hand and said, 'No, no. The wine is for our good host Mr Hare to choose, naturally.'

George could hardly believe he had heard him say this. But everyone was turning towards him and smiling. He looked at the prices on the menu in this expensive restaurant and sat, stunned and appalled. He was, at this point, not yet rich; his agency still very small. And there were currency restrictions, too. His business allowance would not cover this kind of expenditure.

Through a fog of horror, he saw a great dish of lobsters being carried in for Nejat's inspection. Then, the sympathetic face of the one-armed Dane opposite. He leaned forward and said, under cover of neighbouring laughter, 'I am sorry for this. Did you not know? But do not worry too much. We will divide the bill, you and I.'

Even halved, it would be an enormous sum; would take all George had with him, in cash and traveller's cheques. George refused lobster, ordered an egg dish instead, drank only one glass of wine, and raged inwardly. Did he look such a fool, such a sucker? Oh, probably. Nejat had summed him up quite correctly; a mild, English idiot, incapable of protesting in public. He ate his eggs, sipped his wine, worked out sums in his head. Hours seemed to pass. At the head of the table, Nejat stubbed out a cigarette in his barely touched lobster, lifted his glass to George, and drank to him, smiling. 'Now my friend, we will go to a night-club. Drink champagne and dance with the girls.'

George shook his head dumbly. The pale Dane winked at him. He called up the table, 'Only if you will be host, Nejat Bey.'

'But of course! That will be a great honour for me.' Nejat rose, beaming round him. 'I will take all I can in the minibus. You will follow me, please. The place is not easy to find.'

George got out his wallet. The Dane said, 'If you are really poor, I will pay all.' His English was not good enough to put this more tactfully. George forced a smile; shook his head.

The minibus was waiting outside, fully loaded. George found himself, with the Dane, in a dolmus. There were six other men in the shared taxi, all strangers to him, and perhaps to each other, but the driver's dashing style made them, for the space of this journey, intimate as lovers: they swayed thigh to thigh as the taxi screeched up and down the rough, hilly streets and when it came to a sudden, jarring halt, slid forward together onto their knees, as if united in prayer.

They had stopped in a dimly lit, cobbled alley, behind the

minibus. George, last out of the dolmus, was surprised to find that the street seemed at first sight quite empty: his fellow passengers had vanished as if the blank walls either side had opened and swallowed them. He heard running feet and men shouting in Turkish. The noise seemed to be coming from an ancient truck stationed higher up the alley, in front of the minibus. Someone screamed – in rage or in fear. Then the scream was cut off as if a wire had been cut.

George ran up the hill. Nejat was lying on the road between the truck and the minibus with several men round him. One was kneeling on his stomach and another kicking him methodically in the side. Nejat's head was thrown back over the edge of the kerb at an unpleasant angle and he appeared to be gargling.

For a split second George was not displeased with this spectacle. Then he saw blood bubbling from Nejat's mouth. He looked round for help but none of the restaurant party were visible; only the driver of the dolmus, standing by the open door of his vehicle. George shouted, 'Come on,' and then – absurdly, it seemed afterwards – 'Aidez-moi,' and sailed in. He caught the nearest man by the shoulder and in a gesture learned from the cinema screen twirled him round and hit him with his free fist in the throat. The man reeled backwards, retching and choking, and crashed to the ground.

George heard himself laughing exultantly. This absurd, astonishing success had removed the scene from reality. There was no danger here, only pure, slapstick comedy. He danced about, light on his feet as a boy playing at boxing, laughing his madman's laugh and lashing out at the dodging shadows around him. He thought he hit several of them before someone hit him, a sledge-hammer punch on the back of his neck that sent him sprawling. Even then, slithering face downwards along the uneven cobbles, skull exploding with pain, he was still watching himself from afar. He thought, quite dispassionately, *they are going to kill me, no one will stop them, this is the way the world ends* . . .

And was sick with real fear, suddenly. He had fetched up against the side of the minibus, jarring his shoulder. He drew his legs up and threw up his arms to protect his head, but no further blows fell. He waited, sweating and trembling. An engine backfired, then revved noisily. He looked cautiously up and saw the battered truck moving off, two of the men running behind it and trying to clamber aboard as it accelerated up the steep hill.

Nejat was a few yards away, crouching on hands and knees. He was shaking his head and making a growling noise. George got up, staggering, but Nejat was on his feet before he could reach him. He spat something out of his mouth – some of his gold teeth, perhaps? – then lurched drunkenly up the street, waving his arms and shouting, apparently in pursuit of the truck.

George stared after him. Vomit rose in his throat. He leaned over the bonnet of the minibus, coughing and groaning. The Dane said, beside him, 'Are you hurt badly?'

He led George to a dark doorway, down a dark stair into a candle-lit cellar. Excited eyes gleamed in the dimness, hands helped him off with his coat, laid him down on a couch. The Japanese girl was beside him, laying soft, houri's hands on his face. She said, 'They are bringing ice for your eye. You were very courageous. They would have killed Nejat, I think.'

George lay speechless as ice-packs were laid to his swollen cheek. If they believed this, it was incredible that they should all have stood calmly by. Although the Dane could hardly have weighed in, with one arm, there were able-bodied men in the party! But they seemed to feel no embarrassment, crowding round his couch, smiling and toasting him, and when he sat up to drink his first glass of champagne and the band struck up 'Hail the conquering hero', he felt he was the only man in the place to feel shame.

The Dane said, 'Nejat Bey hit the truck with the minibus some time this morning. They must have trailed him all day for revenge.'

'For a *traffic accident*?'

'Apparently Nejat damaged their bumper and refused to pay.'

It seemed an inadequate reason for attempted murder to George. But everyone else appeared to accept it and this increased his bewildered sense of disorientation, of being adrift in some lunatic's dream. It was not until later, during the long hours of a sleepless, pain-filled night, that bewilderment flowed into outrage. By the time morning came, he was buoyantly afloat on a high tide of proud indignation. He went to the Consulate and swept in to see Arthur Bone, flaunting his damaged eye like a decoration.

Arthur listened patiently. He said, 'That's a very nasty cut on your eye, my dear fellow. You should get it seen to. I'll give you the address of my doctor.'

George was deflated. Perhaps this calm man had not fully understood the heroic part he had played. For a moment modesty struggled with what he felt was his due. Then he said casually, 'I thought I should come and tell you what happened in case there was any police trouble. I hit one man pretty hard, after all. Not that I think he's likely to complain. It was amazing, really, the way they all simply ran off! I could hardly have scared them, I never was much of a fighter. Unless they thought I was clean off my head. Madness is always frightening, isn't it? A crazy foreigner, shouting strange oaths!'

Arthur was writing on a memo pad. He tore the sheet off and pushed it across the desk. 'Here you are. He's an excellent chap and speaks good English so you should have no difficulty.'

George said, 'What amazed *me*, of course, was the way all Nejat's so-called friends just disappeared.'

'Perhaps they thought it wiser not to interfere in a private quarrel. If you're sensible you won't either, in future. Unless you want to end up with a knife in your back in the Bosphorus.' He looked at George thoughtfully. 'Nejat is a famous rogue. I should have told you, perhaps.'

George stared, deeply shocked. 'Rogue or not, one could hardly stand by. See him murdered.'

'This is not Samaria,' Arthur Bone said.

Sally said, 'I think that was an awfully cheap, *crappy* thing to say when you'd saved a man's life.'

Her clear voice rang out like a scornful bell. George hushed her, finger to his lips, smiling. They were standing in the Blue Mosque, in the central prayer-hall, slippered feet on rich carpets, the high, marvellous dome soaring above them and dwarfing the small, human absurdities, the vacuum cleaners and grandfather clocks that George had meant to point out to amuse her, but she was too absorbed in her indignation for such minor distractions.

As he was, with her. The sun, streaming in, turned her hair silver, her tanned, shining face, gold. She wore no make-up and her flower-printed dress, long and full in the skirt and high at the neck, was demurely suitable for this occasion: a young girl on a cultural tour of Istanbul with an old friend of her family.

George reminded himself that this was his role. 'Arthur was only doing his duty. It was his job, after all, to safeguard foolish young Englishmen.'

'I don't think you were foolish,' Sally said, softervoiced but still stern. 'I think you were enormously brave.'

'Not really, you know. I just rushed in without thinking. Just didn't know what a dangerous city this was.'

He had thought this was why he had told her the story: to warn her. But the flattered pleasure her reaction had given him revealed his true motive only too clearly: he had wanted her to see him in a youthfully heroic light. Had he planned this while he was dressing this morning? Lips moving in silent rehearsal as he changed a plain shirt for a more fashionable, floral design, chose trousers that clung close to his still slender hips, looked at himself in the glass ... Leila, in bed with a headache, had said, 'You look very nice, George,' and, turning quickly and guiltily, he had caught her smiling at him with prim, secret amusement ...

He said, 'If I'd known it was dangerous, I don't suppose I'd have done it. Certainly I wouldn't now.' He smiled at Sally. 'Older and wiser.'

Her grey eyes reproached him. 'I think you would, George.'

He shook his wise old head, laughing.

She said, sighing suddenly, 'Well, at least you did *once*. Oh, I do envy you! It must be marvellous to know you'd done something like that, if only once in your life. Something that wasn't just selfish, even if it was without thinking. To know you're *capable* of it, that's the thing!' She looked at him, sadly and seriously. 'I hope I would be but I can't *know*, can I, and that frightens me sometimes. Don't laugh, will you? What I mean is, it seems that everything I ever do is for *me*, and it makes me feel – oh, I don't know – small and shrivelled and *lame*. Tied to the ground when I want to fly up. Reach out, touch something. Be part of something important!'

Her eyes looked into dreaming distance and George held his breath. All young girls felt like this probably, immortal longings were just growing pains, but Sally seemed to him, or seemed to his besotted gaze at this moment, to embody and express something deeper, more universal: the sweet, aching desire of the whole human race for some higher purpose, some grand design . . .

She was blushing. He said, 'I know what you mean.'

She laughed at this flat response with an air of relief. He thought that her high-flown sentiments had embarrassed her, once she had uttered them, and she was grateful to him for appearing not to take them too seriously.

She said, bearing this out, 'You are *nice*, George.' And then, over-gaily, laughing, and swinging the silken veil of her hair to cover her face and the ridiculous, crippling shame that had seized her, 'Chance would be a fine thing, wouldn't it? I'm hardly likely to perform any daring deeds staying with Omer. Christ, George, you might have told me the way Turkish girls are expected to behave! The atmosphere is affecting me already – you may observe that my language has moderated. If I stay here much longer I shall be a real ladylike Miss!' She peered up at George, through her shimmering hair, smiling shyly. 'Not allowed to do this, can't do that! Did Omer tell you what happened about Zeynep? I daresay that's partly what makes me feel so frivolous. *She* does, I mean. She's so dedicated.'

'Dedicated to what?'

'Well. Oh, I don't know . . .'

She looked at him doubtfully. He said, 'She's a solemn girl, isn't she?'

She nodded, biting her lower lip, watching him. He smiled. 'Dedicated to herself, shouldn't wonder. But I'm sorry you're disappointed she's not at the villa. I gather there was a bit of a family scene over that.'

'Yes.' She still seemed to be hesitating.

He said, 'Embarrassing for you, I suppose. Were you upset?'

'No. It was interesting, really. An eye-opener. Nili going on as if the world had come to an end because Zeynep wanted to stay in the flat. Who will marry her now? And so on. I couldn't believe it. I said to Omer that I thought it was a disgusting attitude, to assume a girl wasn't virtuous just because she was living alone, and d'you know what he *said*? That I must understand that Turkish women were hot-blooded and Turkish men rather ruthless. He hadn't understood at all what I meant and he's lived in England!'

George found the astonishment with which she said this very endearing.

'Moving round the world doesn't change the way you look at it, necessarily.'

'I thought travel was supposed to broaden the mind.'

'Only in the sense that you've seen more and that can be deceptive. All the tourist gets is a partial view. A bit like watching a film with the sound switched off. You think you know what's going on, you fit your own words to the actions but you may be mistaken.'

'Like being a child in a way. That's a partial view, too.'

'Clever girl.'

'Even if you can hear what the grown-ups are saying you don't always understand it. You get things dreadfully wrong. I remember once, when you were angry with my mother . . .' She giggled and blushed.

'I don't think I've ever been angry with Claire.'

'You were, *then*.' She stopped. 'No – you'll be angry.'

'Don't be silly.' But his pulses had quickened.

'Well. I don't mean it was true, just what it seemed like to me then. You know what it's like when you're young, things go on over your head. I don't know what you were both angry about, but there was this *feeling*. Not just an argument, something much more. As if . . .' She looked at him slyly, and gasped. 'As if you were quarrelling *lovers*.'

'Sally!'

'There, you are angry. I knew you would be.' She started to gabble nervously. 'I don't mean this was *real*; if I did, I wouldn't be telling you, would I? I mean, my parents are so dotty about each other it's quite mawkish, sometimes, and my mother's virtuous enough to please any male Turk. I suppose it's all this rubbishy talk about virtue brought it back now! And I didn't think it, of course, at the time, only when I was older, remembering.' Her eyes shone with mischief. 'When I first fell in love with you. I suppose I was jealous.'

He said, lightly, 'When was this traumatic occasion?'

'Oh, I don't know, exactly. That's a bit much to ask, isn't it?' She frowned for a minute; then went on, slowly, 'I was little. In some sort of pram. You and my mother behind me. Pushing me, I suppose. Talking above me and leaving me out – I remember *that* feeling. And the smell – horrid smell!' She wrinkled her nose up. 'Cat's piss, or something.'

'How extraordinary.'

She looked at him gravely, head on one side. 'Don't you remember something like that? Have I made it all up?'

He made himself smile at her. It seemed to stretch the skin over his skull. He said, 'I'm afraid you must have, my darling.'

Not cat's piss, but lions. A smell of lions . . .

He had taken Claire and Sally to the Zoo. He had just come home after two months away and had gone to see Claire. This bright, autumn afternoon. He was his own master, not a wage-slave, he could take the afternoon off when he chose. And he had chosen to see Claire without Sam. He felt guilty about that. Guilty about Claire, too. He had started to be angry with her in the taxi, partly because he felt guilty.

He had been travelling round Southern Greece with

126

Jane Derby. They had been to Monemvasia where they had shared a room in a small Class B hotel that overlooked the great rock. It was the first time he had been unfaithful to Claire – unfaithful was how he saw it – with someone he was really quite fond of; someone he had thought of marrying. He had told Claire about Jane in the taxi – to unburden himself? Make her jealous? – and she had not answered him. Or not answered immediately. Sitting beside him, her child on her knee, she had looked out of the window. She had had her hair cut and it made her look older and thinner; not a girl any longer.

She turned to him in the end; a grown woman, self-assured, smiling. She said, as if she had been considering this possibility for a long time before he had mentioned it, 'You could do worse than marry Jane, George. I think she'd be right for you.'

He resented her calmness. It seemed to him condescending. He knew what she thought about Jane: a nice girl, but dull. She had once said that; those words exactly. Was that what she thought about *him*? That a nice, dull girl was the sort he should marry?

They had reached the Zoo. He hired a pushchair for Sally. She was too old for a pushchair – how old? Six? Seven? – but she wanted one for some reason. Wanting attention? She stamped her feet, pouting; threatening a tantrum. He said impatiently, 'Let her have one, why not?' She sat in the pushchair, knees drawn up to her chest. Claire said, 'She's spoiled, that's her trouble.'

He was angry with Claire, whom he loved. But he couldn't tell her why he was angry. He said, '*My* trouble is, whenever I think of getting married to someone, I always think, suppose something happened to Sam?' This was a day-dream he often had at this time. He laughed, but he was quite serious. 'I mean, what a mess that would be!'

Claire looked at him. The wind blew her hair round her face like flower petals. She said, 'You mean, if Sam died, you might take up the option?'

'Don't be crude, darling Claire.'

'What you said was crude, wasn't it?'

'It wasn't meant to be. Just an idea that comes into my head, I can't help it. It doesn't mean I want it to happen.'

'Keep it to yourself, then.'

She was angry; as angry as he was. He saw this with surprise and a rising, sexual excitement. She was walking along, shoulders hunched, pushing Sally. He put his hand over hers, on the pushchair, and she shook it off frantically as if an insect had stung her. She said, 'George, *listen*! Once and for all, you haven't any rights over me!'

'*Haven't* I?' she tossed her shorn head. He wanted to shake her till her bones rattled. He said, 'I don't like your hair.'

She looked at him, snorting with laughter. But there were tears in her eyes. He said, 'Darling!' and she shook her head helplessly, bending over the pushchair, saying in an unnatural, arch voice, 'Are you comfy, Sally, screwed up like that? Shall we go and look at the lions? See the big pussies having their tea?'

He followed her into the lion-house. It was feeding time; people crowded the rail, watching the big cats crooning over their bloody meat. A warm, feral stink. He was pushed close to Claire; his arm against hers, feeling her tremble. He said, 'Don't let's quarrel, Claire. Please. It's so silly. Your hair is pretty, once you get used to it. But it makes you look thinner.'

She said, 'I am thinner.'

He looked at her closely. There were lines round her eyes he had not seen before. He said, 'Love, are you all right?'

She nodded.

'You look so pale.'

She was resting against him. He would have put his arm round her waist but she straightened up suddenly, rejecting his tenderness. She said, in a cool, crisp voice, 'I have been ill, I suppose. In a way. I had a miscarriage last month and I still feel a bit groggy occasionally.'

He said, involuntarily, 'Whose child this time?' And then, at once, horrified, 'Oh, Claire. Forgive me, please. That was foul.'

He was too ashamed to look at her face. When he did, finally, he was astonished to see she was smiling. She said, 'Sam's of course,' smiling with clear, innocent eyes. No sign at all that there might have been more to his question than an old friend's privileged teasing except perhaps the slightly heightened gaiety with which she went on, 'It always was possible, George, you know that, just a question of patience! But patience is something I've always been short of, which is why it's such a bloody nuisance it went wrong this time. Not that I care so much for myself, one child's enough for me, I'm not the maternal type, but Sam's unhappy about it and I care about that.'

'I'm sorry.'

'But at least he's got Sally.'

He said, automatically, 'Yes, of course,' looking down at the pale blonde head in the pushchair and thinking, contritely, *poor kid, not much fun for her, she can't see a bloody thing stuck down there*, and then, at that moment, the child twisted round and looked up at him. Hearing her name spoken, probably; luckily the rest of their conversation couldn't have meant much to her. But he felt uneasy all the same, meeting that blank, muddy stare . . .

The mind is an archaeological site. Incidents drop out of conscious memory and lie buried like shards. Lost for years in the rubble. Dig a casual spade's depth down and lord knows what you turn up.

Archaeology – or time travel. Not an artificial device dreamed up by science fiction but the voyages we can all take without leaving our chairs; slipping from childhood to middle life between one breath and another; half a century in a split second. The only ticket you need for this kind of journey is a tone of voice, an evocative smell . . .

Why had he forgotten that scene in the lion-house? Because he came out of it badly? Not his fault if he had: he had been young, still in love with Claire, hurt because he felt she had cheated him. When had he stopped loving her? Then, perhaps: she had shut him out of her life that day, finally. Or later, when he knew he loved Sally?

He thought now – suppose Claire had not lost that baby, suppose she had died, giving birth; no one left to know about Sally, no other witness – and groaned aloud. There was no one to hear him. He was sitting alone on the terrace of the small hotel where he had often stayed in Istanbul in pre-Leila days, looking down over a cardboard tumble of ramshackle streets to the pontoon bridge over the Horn, drinking raki. He had been here over an hour now. He had done his duty by Sally, taken her to three mosques, to lunch at 'Abdullah', to the Topkapi Museum. She was to go back to the villa with Omer on the five o'clock boat. He had sent her to Omer's office in a taxi and walked to this shabby hotel with the deliberate intention of getting steadily and healingly drunk.

Only a temporary refuge, of course, but he needed it badly. Looking at himself, he hadn't much liked what he saw. He was bitter with Claire because she had used him, but he had wanted to be used, hadn't he? There are few un-willing victims in this sort of situation: you get, most of the time, what you ask for. He was a righteous fool to blame

Claire. And a coward, too – hiding from the truth, which was that he had used *her*, knowing that he was quite safe to do so, that he could trust her not to betray him. It might seem a ludicrous game they had played all these years but at least she had played it with style. She had kept her side of the bargain, it was he who had broken it, tormenting her with his love, reproaching her with his guilt, his spoiled life . . .

Why had he done this? Claire – sweet, honourable Claire – had not tied him. He could have broken loose any time; married Jane, married any one of a number of girls. If he'd wanted. Why hadn't he wanted to? Fear of failure? To love Claire, who was unobtainable, was an excuse, a protection.

If you want to know why you fall in love with one particular person at any particular time, you have to look in yourself for the answer. Why did he love Sally now? Love of this grotesquely obsessional kind, socially impossible, incapable of fulfilment, is rarer than poets or novelists (who have a vested interest in it) would have us believe. The truth is, it is an infection healthy people are immune to. Before you catch it, catch this disease, there has to be something wrong, out of balance. Some fatal condition of weakness.

The fault in this case, he decided, lay in the low value he had always placed on himself. He had thought himself worthless, could not see his own life as meaningful. This was why he had clung to Sam as a boy, and later to Sam-and-Claire, drawing vicarious strength from their good and purposeful marriage, twining himself round it like an obstinate parasite round a strong and beautiful tree. Loving Sally was a way to strike his roots deeper.

Recognizing this altered nothing of course. He would not stop loving her. But it suggested a remedy. Now he believed he knew what was wrong he must deal with it, tear out the canker. Put more practically, he must not see

Sally again, or at least not this summer. There was nothing to keep him in Istanbul. One more meeting with Omer, to settle a few final details about their plans for the holiday village, and he would be free to go; free to fly home, or to France, perhaps. Leila was always happy in Paris; would be glad to leave Turkey.

Finishing his raki, he thought of Leila with some apprehension. He had left her alone all day. He had not even telephoned at lunch-time as he had promised he would, to find out if her headache was better. She would be angry and, for once, right to be.

But she didn't seem angry. She was sitting in their room reading a paperback novel. As he came in, she looked up and smiled at him placidly. She was dressed for the evening and had her hair done, back-combed into a high, bouffant style, stiffly lacquered. He thought it looked like an abandoned bird's nest.

He said, 'Your hair looks nice, darling.'

He bent to kiss her, putting his hand on the back of her chair to steady himself.

She said, 'George, you're drunk!'

'Possibly.' Straightening with care, he regarded her warily, but her smile was indulgent. Even a little pleased, as if something she had long expected to happen, had happened at last. He said, 'Yes, you're right. Sorry. Be all right in a minute,' and sank gratefully on to the bed, closing his eyes. The bed tilted beneath him unpleasantly. He felt short of air and there was a high, thin, ringing sound in his head.

Leila's voice reached him from a great distance. 'Don't lie down like that. You'll only feel worse.'

He gave a small moan of acknowledgement. Her cool hands touched his forehead, then slid competently under his shoulders, helping him up. She was sitting beside him, supporting him. Was holding a glass of water. She said, 'Drink as much as you can. It will dilute the alcohol in the blood stream. I'll ring for some coffee.'

She was used, he remembered, to drunkeness. Did she welcome this chance to demonstrate a long unused skill? He was not at all thirsty but he drank the water obediently, to please her, while she telephoned for room service. Then felt sick. He went to the bathroom and crouched over the lavatory, retching and shuddering, clinging to the cool sides of the bowl like a drowning man to a raft. When Leila called to him that the coffee had come he stood up and looked at himself in the mirror with loathing while he washed his hands, rinsed his mouth.

Leila poured coffee. He drank several cups of the black, bitter liquid, scalding his mouth deliberately, as a punishment. He said, 'How utterly repulsive. I'm sorry.'

'Don't mind me, George. I've seen a drunk man before, as you know.' This sort of remark was usually followed by a brief, bitter laugh but her face was smooth and calm beneath her dry nest of hair; her huge eyes shone exultantly. She said, 'Compared with my first husband, you're really quite harmless.'

He tried to match her playful tone. 'I feel too bloody limp to knock you about even if I wanted to.'

'Poor love.'

'No need to be sorry. My own silly fault, after all.'

'I am sorry, though. What you ought to do now, is eat something. If you could manage it, you'd feel better.'

He nodded, though the thought of food nauseated him, and went to shower. She followed him into the bathroom and held his towel ready. He stepped out of the bath and she wrapped it tenderly round him. She said, 'If you sit down on the lavatory seat, I'll dry your feet for you. Bending is *not* recommended for gentlemen in your condition!'

He said, weakly, 'Don't, dear. I can manage. You'll get your pretty dress wet,' but she shook her head, laughing, and knelt at his feet, drying and powdering between his toes as if he were a baby. He let her do it, too surprised at the change in her to protest again. Or was it a change in him? The first time he had appeared before her, defenceless?

He looked down at her bent head and thought, with drunken clarity, that this was the key to what had always been wrong between them. He had never let her do anything for him, never asked anything from her; seeing himself, from the beginning, as the provider, the protector, like the king with the beggarmaid in the old story. King Cophetua, leaning down from his throne and graciously raising the ragged girl up. No one had ever said how *she* felt, being an object of charity . . .

As Leila had been to him. He had married her because he saw her as someone less than himself; someone who would never present any threat to his frail sense of importance. Was this true? Monstrous, if so. But perhaps this was just alcoholic remorse. He was not utterly loathsome. He meant to meet his debts, however inadequately.

He said, loudly, 'I do love you, you know,' and she looked up at him, frowning. He wondered at the frown and then realized she had been saying something and he had interrupted. He said, 'I'm sorry.'

She put one hand on the bath and stood up. Her face, healthily flushed, swam above him.

'I was only saying, what happened to Sally? Omer rang up. He was expecting her at the office, apparently.'

She was picking his clothes up, discarding some, folding others. The bathroom was full of steam; she rubbed at the looking glass over the basin with the sleeve of his shirt and looked at her reflection, touching her hair anxiously.

He said, 'What time was this?'

'I'm not sure. About five, I think. I'd just come back from the hairdresser.'

'She should have been with him by four-fifteen at the latest. I put her in a taxi.'

His shocked tone seemed to amuse her. She shrugged her shoulders and gave a little, purse-lipped, superior smile. 'Don't look so worried, George. Fuss, fuss, fuss – like an old hen with one chick!'

He stared at her. 'Where would she go?' He was asking himself this question, not Leila. And thought he knew the answer.

'How should I know? Shopping or something. You know what girls are. She's not a baby. Perhaps she was fed up with being treated like one.'

He got up from the lavatory seat, pushed past her into the bedroom, and began to dress. His mind, which had been full of thin, drifting thoughts, like wisps of smoke, had cleared miraculously. He should have known something like this was likely to happen. She had probably planned it. The first opportunity she had had to escape Omer's vigilance! Oh – he should have guessed something was up from her manner. All that false meekness!

Leila said, 'Naturally, when Omer telephoned, I assumed she was still with you. That's what I told him. I said to go home himself, not to worry, you'd look after her. See her on the boat, or bring her back here with you.'

'I'd have let him know if I was going to do that, wouldn't I? I knew he'd be waiting.'

'You might have lost count of time.' She laughed, with faint malice.

'Don't be absurd.'

'Well, what was I to think? You weren't here, you hadn't rung. It was the obvious thing. Then, when you came in, you were in no condition . . .'

'I know. I'm sorry.'

'I just forgot to tell you.'

'Yes. It wasn't your fault.'

'Thank you.' She laughed again, but with a trace of uneasiness now. 'What's the time?'

He was fastening his watch on his wrist. He looked at it. 'Twenty to seven.'

'That's not late.'

'No.'

'What could happen to her, in broad daylight?'

'Nothing, I hope. I'm sorry if I seem to be fussing. I think I know where she's probably gone. To Omer's flat to see Zeynep.'

As soon as he had said this aloud, he felt eased: there was nothing mysterious here, only a girl playing truant. He smiled at this thought. 'Omer wouldn't be pleased if he knew, but one can hardly blame Sally. Natural that she should want to spend some time with her friend. And she's not used to being locked up, like a child in a nursery.'

Leila said, severely, 'I'm afraid, if you ask me, I do blame her, George. She should have told Omer what she was doing. She's his guest, after all. I think you should ring him.'

'And say what? He thinks she's with us, doesn't he? So there's no point in worrying him. Not unnecessarily.' He laughed. 'Old Omer likes to guard his peace.'

'Would he really be worried? Or are you just saying that because you want me to think there's some cause to be?' Leila reddened suddenly, stretching her neck. 'Oh, it's a good excuse, isn't it?'

He noted the flush but was too preoccupied to analyse this threateningly cryptic remark. Thinking – *Sally's not rude.* If she had intended to give Omer the slip and spend the night with Zeynep, she would have rung him herself. Unless something was wrong. 'An excuse?' he said vaguely.

'Oh, George, George . . .' She shook her head, wearily sighing – she could explain what she meant if she had to, but preferred to hold back, out of delicacy! She was still holding his clothes, picked up in the bathroom. She looked at them now as if wondering what she was doing with this stranger's trousers, his shirt, and put them down on the bed. Then raised her eyes to his face. In spite of her stagey behaviour they seemed dull with some genuine pain. She said, carefully, 'If you feel you should go and see she's all right, please don't let any concern for me stop you.'

Chapter 7

It was almost dark. Walking from the hotel, he had watched the slender spires of a mosque grow black against a red sky. Lights were on in the house and in Omer's family flat, on the first floor, the lit windows of the main room were open on to the balcony. George knew that room intimately. Between the two long windows there was a glass fronted display-case containing what Omer called, proudly, his 'Atatürk Museum'. Letters sent to his father from Atatürk, medals, a signed photograph, a lock of Atatürk's hair, set in a gold brooch, like a saint's relic.

Omer had showed George these things the last time he had been in Istanbul. That had been a year ago; a cold spring, the city lashed with bitter rain. Since then, the next door building had been demolished, laid flat as a bomb site, except for a single tree round which children were playing in the last of the light: boys perched in the branches like birds. A low wind blew along the ground, chilly suddenly, whipping up yellow dust. George had the taste of grit in his mouth.

He stood, watching the flat, in the doorway of the house opposite. He was not conspicuous: there was a hairdressing salon in the basement and a small shop beside it. People were coming and going. A man, pushing a barrow piled high with white strawberries, stopped on the steep hill in front of George, to draw breath and cough.

Sally appeared on the balcony. She was wearing a dark scarf over her hair and a dark jacket hiding her dress. The sleeves of the jacket were too long for her, falling over her hands as she leaned on the iron railing and looked up the street.

The man with the fruit-barrow rested the handle against his chest, took a cigarette out of his shirt pocket, lit it, inhaled deeply, coughed with a wet, desperate sound. Sally glanced down at him briefly, then went back into the room.

George thought – what I am waiting for?

Like a comment on his indecision, a taxi, swerving violently into the narrow street, missed the barrow by a hair's breadth and stopped on its far side, completely blocking the roadway. Another taxi and a small van were behind it. They squealed to a halt and their drivers put their hands on their horns and left them there to wail in indignant cacophony. The driver of the first taxi got out, shouting something in Turkish – explanation or abuse, perhaps both – and opened his boot. Another man appeared and helped him to load a large box, or trunk, into it. This took perhaps thirty seconds during which the noise level rose to what might, in another city, be considered beyond human endurance, as windows opened blaring out radio music in dispute with the horns and lookers-on yelled advice or encouragement. The driver slammed down the lid of the boot, returned to his seat, slammed the door.

George, laughing, his hands over his ears, saw that Sally was in the back of the taxi. Her face, unfamiliarly framed in the dark, enveloping scarf, seemed to him anxious and pale.

He called, 'Sally!' and although she could not possibly have heard his voice, thought she turned towards him. But the car was moving already. He dodged round the fruit-barrow and grabbed at the door of the second taxi. The driver was young, ruddy-faced, with fine, bold, dark eyes and a neat, black moustache.

George said, 'Would you follow my friend in that taxi?'

The man looked at him blankly. He couldn't know why George was laughing, unless he had seen the same old American films. Perhaps not even then. What was the Turkish phrase for *follow that car*?

The driver said, 'Feri-bot.' Not a question, a statement. Perhaps the other man had explained why he was holding the traffic up: his passengers were in a hurry to get to the ferry?

George nodded. There seemed no alternative. He fell back in the seat as the taxi shot off down the hill and took a sharp left turn past the flattened building site. It was quite dark now but some of the boys remained in the tree, their white shirts glimmering like pale, folded wings.

The driver said, 'American?'

'English,' George answered sharply. This familiar assumption always annoyed him.

'Manchester?'

'No, London. Why, do you know someone from Manchester?'

'Please?'

'Never mind.'

The lights of the Bosphorus twinkled beneath them. There were other cars racing towards it. This was the road that led to the ferry. Was Sally intending to take it? Even if she were, what was he doing, racing after her? So infatuated any excuse would do was what Leila thought and he had nothing to put against this except a vague, suspicious ache in his mind that now seemed pure melodrama. All that had happened was that Sally had gone to see Zeynep, as he had expected she might, and now she was going somewhere else. What was wrong with that? Perhaps Zeynep was with her and they were crossing the Bosphorus to visit friends, go to a party.

He sat in the swaying taxi with an almost amused sense of

defeat. Even if he caught up with Sally, what could he say to her? Dress her down for not telling him, this afternoon, where she was going?

They stopped on the water-front in a long line of cars. Already, the first in the queue had begun to bump up the gangway on to the boat. George's driver jerked on his brakes, got out of the taxi, and ran up the line for his ticket. George got out too and peered helplessly along the crowded quay. All Istanbul taxis looked alike to him: a uniform air of decrepitude.

The boat's siren blew a mournful warning and the driver came running back, waving his ticket and wearing a broad grin of heroic achievement. He caught George's arm and propelled him back to the car. He said, 'Quick, we go now. Next feri-bot twenty minutes.'

They edged slowly forwards. George said, 'Is the other taxi on the ferry?' and the man shrugged his shoulders, perhaps not understanding this question. George sat back, resigned. Once on board, he could look for Sally. If he didn't find her, he would return on the same boat, go back to the hotel and telephone Omer. He found himself cravenly hoping for this simple solution.

They were the last car on the ferry, jammed in so tight it was impossible to open the doors. A high van on one side, the boat rail on the other. The driver said, 'I am sorry, no room. But it is not a great journey.' This came out easily: it was an apology, perhaps, he had often to make.

George said, 'It doesn't matter.' He rolled the window down and felt the cold air sting his cheek. The boat moved, throbbing, across the Bosphorus.

The driver rested one arm on the back of his seat and smiled at George radiantly. 'Good city, 'Stanbul?'

George nodded.

'From Ankara, I.'

George smiled.

The man said, 'At home I have . . .' His English deserted him. He flapped one hand in the air and said, 'Zzzzz.' His handsome, dark eyes watched George anxiously.

George said, 'Bees?' The man looked doubtful. George lifted his arms in the shape of a cone. 'Bees,' he repeated. 'Buzz, buzz. Hive. Honey.' He rubbed his stomach and smacked his lips.

The driver laughed with delight. 'Honey! Yes, I have honey.' He reached under the dashboard, brought out a small, round, white carton and offered it to George with a little bow. 'Honey. For you.'

George shook his head, smiling.

The man said impatiently, 'Yes, yes, for you. Not for sell. For you. For my friend.'

George took the carton. It was very sticky. He said, 'Thank you very much.'

'Good honey.'

'I'm sure it is.'

'Please?'

'It is good honey.'

'Yes.'

They beamed at each other awkwardly, trapped in mutual goodwill as they were trapped in the car. A soldier released them, tapping brusquely on the driver's window and demanding his papers. There was barely room between the car and the van. He stood, uncomfortably wedged, examining the documents very slowly and carefully by the light of a small pencil torch. When he had finished he shot the beam inside the taxi, shining it blindingly into George's eyes. The driver said something in Turkish and the soldier laughed and snapped off the torch.

When he had gone George said, 'Bloody soldiers!' and grinned with a hint of conspiracy.

The driver did not respond. His eager, mobile face had gone suddenly dead – as if a blind had been drawn across a lit window. He said, 'They keep peace,' and turned, presenting his back to George like a deliberate rebuke. He switched on the radio and a blare of music filled the car.

The motion of the boat had changed. It drew shudderingly alongside the shore. George could see a group of soldiers standing outside a café on the quay. One, an officer, was drinking from what looked like a lemonade bottle. When the gangway was secured, he moved towards it, tossing the bottle away and laughing like a boy.

Last on the boat, George's taxi disembarked first. The soldiers stopped it, thumping the bonnet and motioning the driver to draw to one side. He produced his papers again and the laughing officer looked at them casually, as if this were a game he was playing; then walked round the car, kicking the tyres.

George wrapped the carton of honey in his handkerchief and put it, with some reluctance, into his pocket. He sat watching the boat. The Army appeared to be making a good-tempered, random check: most vehicles were being waved on. Sally's among them. He saw the taxi jerk down on to the quay with a sense of amazement and knew he had not really expected to see it; that if he had, he would have got out and waited at the foot of the gangway. There was no time for that now. He saw the car, recognized the driver and the girl sitting beside him, and Sally's bobbing, scarfed head in the back; then it was past and gone, accelerating up the road to the left.

The officer was talking to his driver. It seemed to be a social conversation. George cleared his throat and they both looked at him with surprise as if he had, up to now, been invisible. The officer moved back, lifting his hand in farewell. George said, pointing, 'Along that road, please.'

'Night-club.'

George hesitated. 'I'll see. I'll tell you when to stop.'

The man sighed, but briefly. The incomprehensible behaviour of foreigners was his bread and butter. Or perhaps he was not, after all, so very happy in the presence of soldiers and the officer was still watching the car. He put it into gear and moved off, past the café and the Army checkpoint, up the winding, corniche road.

There were villas on both sides, secluded behind bougainvillaea and high, iron gates. This was Asia, but in the soft, scented dark, it could have been Surrey. Any comfortable suburb full of prosperous people. But Sally was not going to one of these villas, wearing that clumsy, concealing jacket and scarf. If he caught up with her at all, it would probably be at some small café at one of the villages along the coast. The driver might know a likely place but it seemed unwise to ask: wherever his sympathies lay, it would not be with students. The rich and secure, like Omer, could afford to be indulgent towards their dangerous young: the poor preferred peace.

He saw them before he expected to, before they reached the first village. The road wound up to a small headland where there was a paved picnicking area overlooking the Bosphorus: wooden tables and benches placed beneath sheltering trees. The taxi was parked off the road and Zeynep and the driver were standing beside it. They seemed to be arguing: the man was gesturing, as if angry. George could not see Sally.

His car swept past. He waited until they had negotiated several more bends and then said, loudly and firmly, 'This house here, please.'

It was a large villa, set back, with a broad driveway where the taxi could turn. The gates were closed but well lit. The man stopped and waited in silence while George got out and paid him. Offended? Or frightened because George had insulted the Army? George wished he could say something, make some gesture to recall the moment of friendship they had shared on the boat, but the handsome young face was sullen and remained so even when he saw the tip George had given him. He had offered his friendship, as he had offered his honey, for nothing.

George waited while he turned the car; watched the lights disappear, standing in the shelter of a dark bush beside the high gate. It smelt of something familiar; he broke a leaf in his fingers and knew what it was. Ginger cake. A daphne bush, smelling of ginger cake.

He walked back down the road with this homely scent in his nostrils and an odd, exultant fear in his mind. He had lived so long as a tourist, seeing only mosques and minarets, the ruins of ancient cities, dug over and labelled for visitors, abandoned cultures preserved in the clean shops of selected hotels. Choosing the partial view both for profit – how much money had he made out of this postcard world? – and for his own comfort: reality was dirt and danger and muddle and he preferred pretty pictures, tidied-up landscapes looked at from an air-conditioned coach window.

Well, he was out of the coach now, alone on the road. He laughed and thought – *Am I still slightly drunk?*

The taxi had gone. The girls were still there. The box that had been in the boot of the car stood under the trees. A tin trunk, dark in the moonlight.

He said, 'Sally.'

Her face shocked him. So pale – stupid with terror. He said, 'What's going on?' in a loud, hearty voice and she started to cry. She ran at him, stumbling and crying like a hurt, frightened child. He put his arms round her and looked at Zeynep, over her shoulder.

Zeynep said, 'Please take her away, will you?'

He said, 'What's she doing here, anyway?'

'I didn't invite her.'

'No?'

'She turned up at the flat. I had an appointment and she wanted to come. Why should I stop her?'

'I can't answer that, can I? You might have thought she'd be useful.'

'If I did think that, I was wrong. She wanted to help me. Then she got scared when the pig of a driver turned nasty.'

Sally shuddered in his arms, pressing her face into his shoulder. He put his hand on the back of her head and held it protectively. He said, 'In what way?'

'He wanted to know what I had in my luggage. Seeing the soldiers on the boat made him – sensitive.' She chose this word carefully, then looked at him. 'I told him it was only my books but he wouldn't believe me.'

'And put you off here? Why didn't you open the trunk?'

Her eyelids drooped in the offensive way he remembered. This was a foolish question, not worth answering.

He said, dry with anger, 'All right, I don't want to know. It's none of my business, thankfully.' He felt guilty at once, saying this. He went on, 'Look, I don't know what you're up to, though I can make a rough guess, but I'll help if I can. If you've got involved in some silly mess . . .'

Sally began to laugh hysterically. He held her away from him, gripping her shoulders, and shook her. He said, 'Shut *up*, will you?' in a low, savage voice, and she gasped, closing her eyes and collapsing against him. He helped her to a bench and she sat on it, limp as a doll, head lolling, feet dragging sideways.

Zeynep said, 'There's no mess. I'm taking some things to a friend. All you can do is take Sally away with you.'

She had spoken with what seemed simple, social impatience. Doubt immobilized him.

'We can't leave you here, on the road.'

'Why not? I'm all right. There will be another taxi along in a minute. Or my friends will come looking for me.'

'What friends?'

'Not the sort you'd want Sally mixed up with.'

Sally whispered, 'Please . . .' She was rocking from side to side, dragging her knuckles down her cheeks like a despairing old woman. They stood, looking at her. In the silence they could hear music from the café down by the ferry and the low grind of a vehicle beginning the long climb up the hill.

'It doesn't matter to me what you do,' Zeynep said. 'But if I were you, I'd get her out of this, while you can.'

He thought her voice shook. She was very young, after all, and certainly frightened.

He said, 'You could come with us. Leave that bloody trunk, whatever it is. You're an American citizen, aren't you? I can take you straight to the Embassy.'

She shook her head.

'What will you do then? Hope for a miracle? That driver may have gone straight to the police. That may be them coming now.'

She smiled at him suddenly. It was the first time he had seen her smile, he realized. He listened to the sound of the engine labouring uphill towards them and felt caught up in one of those nightmares of childhood, in which you know some unspecified danger will appear in a minute, from behind the closed door or out of the cupboard, and you can do nothing to stop it.

But it was only an old bus that came round the corner, moaning in bottom gear. Sally got up from the bench and ran wildly away from the road towards the edge of the cliff. He thought for a second she meant to throw herself over and ran after her, catching her arm and jerking her backwards. She shouted something he didn't hear and he pulled her against him, covering her mouth with his hand. The bus passed them and drew up beside Zeynep. She stood on the step and spoke to someone inside. The bus was panting like an exhausted animal, belching out evil black smoke. Two men in dark hats got out and loaded the trunk into the luggage compartment. Zeynep watched them.

George stood, shielding Sally, but no one looked in their direction. The men climbed back into the bus and Zeynep followed them without one backward look. If she had looked, George thought, he could not have stood there. That was a coward's excuse. Though what could he have done? He thought, with a deeper sense of despair than he had ever encountered before – *This isn't Samaria*.

The bus moved off. Sally was quiet in his arms. He released her and said in a cold, neutral voice, 'We'll walk back to the ferry. Take off your scarf. And that jacket.'

She obeyed him. Her eyes watched him mutely. He put the scarf in his pocket, felt the sticky carton of honey, took it out and threw it into the bushes at the side of the road. He folded the jacket inside out and hung it over his arm.

She stood in front of him, her head bowed. In her light, cotton dress, pale hair flowing, she looked flowery and summery. A young English girl.

He said, 'I'm sorry if you're cold but you'll have to put up with it. I don't want you recognized on the ferry. Did that taxi-driver get a good look at you?' She didn't seem to understand this. He sighed. 'Sally. Did you talk to the driver?'

She shook her head. Her dumbness enraged him. He said, 'For bloody Christ's sake, you got yourself into this, didn't you?'

She was shivering like a wet dog. He took her arm, controlling his anger, trying to keep his voice conversational. 'If we walk, you'll get warm. Try and tell me what happened. I have to know, don't I? If I'm to help you.'

He marched her briskly along. After a minute she said in a soft, toneless voice, 'I went to see Zeynep. She didn't know I was coming. I didn't mean to stay. Just to see her . . .'

'Yes?'

'She didn't *want* me to stay. But she was feeling so awful. She had a bad curse-pain. She often does, she has a rotten time that way. I thought that was all that was wrong but in the end she told me she had this – this thing to do, and I said that I'd help her. Go with her to the other side of the ferry anyway. Someone was meeting her there. But we saw the soldiers and she asked the taxi to go on a bit, up the coast. . .'

She stopped, drawing a long shaky breath, and looked at him helplessly.

'And he got suspicious? Oh God, Sally, weren't you? Did you really think this was how a girl like Zeynep normally spent her evenings? Carting a load of school books from Europe to Asia?'

'I don't know.'

'I don't believe you. I simply do not believe you. No one could be so bloody naïve.'

But they could, of course. What did she know about Turkey? He could have told her. But he had been too busy boasting; pandering to his middle-aged sexual vanity.

She said miserably, 'I don't know what I thought, really. It wasn't unreasonable. I mean, some books aren't allowed here and she said she was afraid the flat might be searched. I thought – I *think* I thought – that this sounded a bit cloak and dagger, but I wanted to help her. I knew she belonged to an – an organization, and she had to do certain things. What she was told, without questioning what it was. Even if it seemed a bit silly, a bit like a game, it wasn't to her. It was a *discipline*. She believed it was right and I admired her for that. But I wouldn't have gone with her if she hadn't felt ill. Nor if I'd known . . .' She started to shake again, 'I didn't know, George . . .'

He stopped walking and swung her round to face him. He said, 'Oh, my sweet Christ! Didn't know *what*? Look at me, Sally. You didn't know that it wasn't proscribed literature she was taking to her chums? Not books, but guns, is that it? And when she did tell you, you collapse in a fit of the vapours like a Victorian miss?'

She was shaking her head. Her mouth had gone soft and loose; her eyes stared at him blankly.

He said, slowly and evenly, 'You – fucking – stupid – little – bitch.' She gasped as if he had doused her with cold water and started to smile. He said, 'I'm glad you find it so bloody funny. They hang people who supply terrorists with guns, in this country.'

'It's not guns. It's a body. A dead man.'

She was still smiling that fixed silly smile. He felt cold with shock and then thought – She's covering up! Ashamed of her hysteria and covering up, as a child might, with desperate invention. He said, sharply, 'Don't tell silly lies.'

His tone seemed to calm her, like a slap in the face. She said, 'Perhaps she was lying. She wanted me to leave her and walk back to the ferry and I wouldn't. I was too scared. That's when she told me. It seemed true then, now it seems it can't be. Like waking up from a nightmare.'

He stared at her. She said with sudden, pitiful hope, 'She wanted to get rid of me. Could it be that? She was telling me this awful lie just to get rid of me?'

'What else did she say?'

'That they'd shot this man because he refused to obey an order. She said they'd shoot her if she disobeyed now. It can't be true, can it?'

'I don't know.'

He felt heavy and stupid; too tired to be frightened. Or

perhaps the situation was too unbelievable. A sense of un-reality can act like a tranquillizer. He said, 'I must say I find it hard to believe. But there's no point in speculation. We can't help her, anyway. All we can do at this moment is get you safely back on the ferry. I'll take you to the hotel for the night and we'll see what to do in the morning. Don't talk anymore. Try not to think.'

He took her arm and led her down the road. She came with him passively. They turned the next bend and saw the lights of the ferry beneath them and several cars waiting. The soldiers were still outside the café, talking and laughing. He felt her tremble and said, 'It's all right. I'm here to look after you. Just hold on to that and keep walking. No one will bother us.' He wished he could be certain of that. He laced his fingers in hers and made himself smile at her con-fidently. 'Trust me, darling.'

There were taxis parked on the quay. Was her driver among them? Better not think about that. But they would have to pass the taxis to get on the ferry.

She said, 'What'll happen?'

'Nothing, with luck.'

'I mean, to her. If they catch her.'

'Perhaps they won't. Don't think about it.'

'They do terrible things. She told me. One of her friends . . .'

'I know what they do. Everyone knows. It doesn't help to talk about it.'

'I ought not to have left her.'

'She didn't want you.'

'Only because I was acting so stupidly. Before that, I was useful. She said so. Two girls together are less suspicious than one. I could *still* be useful if anything happens. I know she's been made use of, I could explain that, how it happened, *everything*. It might make a difference.'

'I very much doubt it.'

She said stubbornly, 'They'd have to listen to me!'

Her innocence terrified him. Here and now it was especially dangerous. If there was another Army block further along the coast, they might have stopped the bus already; searched the luggage compartment . . .

A car drew up behind them, pooping its horn, and his heart jumped in his throat.

Arthur Bone said, 'My dear George.'

Two kind, horsey faces regarded him curiously. They had been driving with the roof down and Arthur's white hair, blown by the wind, looked like a fine, silken mane. Mary wore a dark, man's felt hat, that was too large for her, tied beneath her chin with a tattered length of black chiffon.

'Can we give you a lift, my dears?' Arthur said.

They sat in the car, on the ferry. No one had stopped them. Arthur had put the roof up, for privacy, and it was stiflingly hot. Sally was in the back with Mary Bone who had her arm round her. She had whimpered once or twice while George talked, but now she was silent.

As Arthur had been all the time. Listening intently, not interrupting. Now he said, 'She mustn't go back to Omer, that's the first thing. Zeynep has been living in his flat. Even if he weren't already known for his liberal sympathies, he'll automatically be under suspicion. He can't protect Sally.'

He drummed his fingers on the steering wheel and looked calmly thoughtful, as if the problem he was considering, though undeniably awkward, was basically a minor one. He cleared his throat and sighed. 'The best course, if it can be managed, would be to send her home straightaway.'

'I'm not a *parcel*,' Sally said. But she was sounding frightened.

Arthur turned in his seat and smiled at her kindly. 'No.

Simply a tedious nuisance to everyone. To my mind, what you did was no more than exceptionally childish and silly, but the police here will take a quite different view and I can't say I blame them. You might well go to prison, and that would not be a grand martyrdom but an extremely disagreeable experience that could go on for rather longer than you would find interesting. And without helping anyone.'

Sally blushed darkly. Her humiliation was so pitiful that it hurt George to look at her.

He said, 'She's innocent, Arthur.'

'Only relatively, my dear. Would you want her questioned?'

George felt sick. The car seemed quite airless.

Arthur said, 'They may not wish to, of course. The Turkish government have been embarrassed enough recently. By that wretched British boy they sentenced for peddling drugs. Quite rightly in my opinion – all that xenophobic fuss in the British press was both misinformed and ridiculous – but it's made them sensitive here. That could cut both ways. But I think they'd be anxious not to make a mistake.'

George said slowly, 'You're assuming they'll pick up Zeynep tonight? And find out there were two girls, not one?'

'One has to assume it. Prepare for the worst, and hope it won't happen.'

'And you really do think she told Sally the truth? That there was a dead man in that trunk and she'd killed him?'

Sally said, 'She didn't kill him. Someone else did. They shot him in the flat last night and she was told to get rid of him.' Her voice was flat and astonished. She couldn't believe what she was saying.

George couldn't believe it either. He said, 'It's *grotesque*.'

Arthur laughed his soft, whinnying laugh. 'My dear, these things do happen. If one looks at it sensibly, the only really grotesque thing is that one is so seldom involved in them!'

Chapter 8

Sally slept. She lay on Leila's bed, one hand under her cheek, the other lost in the stiff swirl of her skirt. Her long, bare, brown feet were crossed at the ankles and gracefully pointed. She looked like an exhausted ballet dancer.

George thought – what shall I tell Sam? And felt numb with guilt. He should have known Zeynep was dangerous. It seemed now he had known but had chosen not to acknowledge it. Oh, not 'chosen', perhaps. It was the way his mind always worked: his unconscious tunnelling away in the dark like a busy mole, examining clues, reassessing opinions, throwing up facts like jigsaw pieces until hindsight forced him to fit them together. He imagined himself telling Sam this, and Sam's answer. 'Rather a hit-and-miss method, old boy.' Though not blaming him. Sam never blamed anyone.

They had once had their bicycles pinched on a camping holiday, their last year at school. It had been George's job to padlock them together and he had forgotten to do so. When he woke in the morning and found they were gone he cursed himself savagely, then crawled into the tent to tell Sam, still asleep, and sat looking down at him curled up in his sleeping-bag, reluctant to wake him. Sam's bike was precious to him, representing a year of odd jobs on Saturdays, and George thought of his disappointment with an almost physical pain, heightened by the knowledge that Sam wouldn't reproach him.

People changed, though. Perhaps his picture of Sam was out of date, like an old photograph? He had not really looked at him for years, George realized suddenly, except as Claire's husband, Sally's father. His *rival*. Not as Sam himself; as the boy he'd grown up with and achingly loved, sleeping once in a shared tent on a bicycling holiday, hand under his cheek, as Sally slept now . . .

A deep, drunken sleep. Arthur had driven them back to the hotel and insisted that they all dine together. It was – amazingly to George – only eleven o'clock and the dining-room was still open. 'A little conspicuous gaiety would not come amiss,' Arthur said. 'The end, you see, of a jolly and innocent evening. Not much of an alibi, but better than nothing.'

George had protested – they had done quite enough, why should they involve themselves further? – but the Bones smiled at him calmly and kindly. 'Arthur and I always eat late in hot weather,' Mary said. 'Why don't you ring Leila, Arthur dear, and ask her to join us?'

Arthur telephoned from the desk. His high voice rang out clearly. 'My dear, I know it's disgracefully late but I hope you'll forgive us . . . Oh, yes, George is with us, and Sally . . . We've been on a little drive and we thought we would round off the evening. Please come down, won't you? Mary and I are so longing to see you.'

They were alone in the dining-room. The Bones set about producing all the signs of a convivial party, with what seemed the simple determination of elderly children intent on enjoying themselves. When Leila appeared, they greeted her with loud cries of pleasure – 'My dear, how nice!', 'Isn't this *fun!*' – and seated her between them. George was afraid their enthusiasm might look excessive, even to Leila, but he had misjudged the extent of their skill. Mary asked her what she had seen and done since they last met and listened to her answers with courteous gravity, as if they contained information of startling value. 'It is so important for people like Arthur and me to hear first impressions. The fresh, un-cluttered view. Living in a country, one gets stale sometimes, without knowing it.' Arthur poured wine and flattered her with a lumbering, old-fashioned charm, raising his glass, roguishly, 'to your bright eyes, my dear', making her blush and laugh and glance at George with a sly, triumphant air, as if to say, *You see? I am a success with some of your friends, whatever you say*.

It saddened him that they should have summed her up so well. But it would have been a sentimental luxury, at this moment, to find her pitiable. Her egotism distracted atten-tion from Sally, who sat silent, drinking steadily but hardly touching her food, and her ignorance, George saw, was a form of security. He said – speaking loudly, for the benefit of whatever police spies Arthur imagined might be lurking among the tired waiters in this empty dining-room – 'Sally did miss the boat, after all. Too intent on sightseeing. The hotel's booked solid, so she'll have to squeeze in with us for the night, I'm afraid.'

This sounded theatrically stilted, he thought, like a learned speech in some foolish charade. But Arthur was nodding and beaming as if congratulating him on playing his unexacting part unexpectedly well.

'Or she could come home with us,' he said. 'Couldn't she, Mary? We've no guest-room, but there is a quite comfortable couch in my study.'

Sally made a sudden, jerky movement and knocked her glass over. She stared at the spreading wine stain and said in an agonized voice, 'Oh, how clumsy. I'm sorry.'

George said, 'It doesn't matter, my darling.'

The blood rose in Sally's cheeks. Leila looked at him and then laughed in an amused and knowing way that chilled him. For a horrified moment he thought she was about to make some fantastic accusation – that he had intended this to happen, had been planning, all along, some wild, sexual orgy. But all she said was, 'Oh, there's no need to put you and Mary out, Arthur. We can manage. We have a simply enormous room with two double beds in it. And the child looks dead tired.'

His instinct had been right, though. Leila could turn almost any situation into a comedy of the crudest kind. He had been wondering what – how much? – he should tell her but it was clear as soon as Sally collapsed on the bed, into sleep, that any explanation would be received as an insult. She removed Sally's sandals and straightened her skirt with the tender delicacy any woman might show to another – showing George, at the same time, that her quarrel was with him, not with this innocent girl – then beckoned him on to the balcony. He saw her eyes, bright with righteous excitement, but even then he could not really believe she was about to embark on one of her scenes – reality, just now, was farcical enough without this addition – and her first words fell on his ears with the unreverberating sound of an only half-understood foreign language.

'It's late, George, and I'm far too tired for a lot of discussion. I'm afraid I haven't your stamina. But I must say this one thing. It may seem petty and shallow to you, but I'm sorry, it's still important to me. And it's this. However you treat me privately, please, in future, don't humiliate me in front of your friends, make a fool of me as you have just done this evening. Parading your infatuation for that child as if you were proud of it – as if it showed what a fine fellow you were! They don't admire you for it, whatever you think. They were simply as embarrassed as I was.'

'Leila, darling . . .'

Half-laughing, incredulous, he put a hand on her shoulder but she shook it off and stepped back with an air of revulsion. Her face was marble-pale, her mouth a dark smudge, her eyes tragic caverns.

'Don't *darling* me, if you please. Such hypocrisy – I could vomit! *Sally's* your darling! Do you think I'm quite blind? Oh, I *have* been, a silly, blind fool, but my eyes are open now. And what I see hurts me. Not just for my own sake, but for your sake as well. It's so idiotic. *You're* idiotic, George. A foolish, doting old man, capering about after a girl half your age. Pretending to me you were worried about her, when the truth was you simply couldn't bear to let her out of your sight. I don't know what you were up to this evening, and I don't want to know, thank you, but I won't be used any longer. You've done enough, George, I've come to the end of my tether. Dragging your friends into it, making me dance attendance! Why did you do that? To show off? Or to make them think *I* didn't mind your shenanigans; that we were a happy threesome together? Oh, that puts the tin lid on it!'

'Please, Leila,' he said. 'Please, Leila. Listen.'

But he knew it was useless. She had pointed herself, like a missile, in her chosen direction and nothing he could say would make her change course. Her aim was destruction and she did not want to be diverted: if she could not have perfection, she would have nothing. A kind of perversity that might seem like madness but which arose out of a great reservoir of despair. Out of fear, too – she was obsessed by the fear of being unregarded, alone – but this she would never admit, could not bear to. Preferring to connive at her own defeat. Go down shouting.

He saw this suddenly, with absolute clarity. Saw too, that there was nothing he could do, no way he could help her. The only therapy that eased her at all were these outbursts of violence. And they were not simply a matter of letting off steam, of setting free poisonous gases, but a positive act of creation. Passionate and protesting, flashing eyes and thundering heart, Leila was an artist in her element; channelling and controlling her anger into the shape and rhythm of a work of art.

She was slowing down now: he heard the change in her voice like a car shifting gear. '. . . so don't say listen Leila, listen Leila, to me anymore; it's time the boot was on the other foot, don't you think? I'm older than you, George, too old for all this emotion, and not only in years. My life has never been easy and it's left its mark on me, scars and wounds that I try my best to keep hidden because it's true what they say, laugh and the world laughs with you, weep and you weep alone, and the last thing I want to be is a skull at the feast, not at yours, anyway, because even though you won't believe it, I've meant to be a good wife to you, not a millstone. I knew when we married that all that lovey-dovey stuff couldn't last, that I'd have to face something like this sometime in our lives, but I'd prepared myself for a discreet affair or two when I was older and uglier, I never thought it would happen so soon nor that it would be something like this. The male menopause, the Lolita complex, I suppose that's how one sums it up – comic, really! We ought to be laughing but I can't at this moment. It's not that I mind for myself, even though I feel I'm bleeding to death, I know it'll pass. I'm tough, I wouldn't have survived this long if I hadn't been. I'd have put my head in the gas-oven. I nearly did once, d'you know that? After Roland had left me. Not that he was any great loss but I felt so alone and my mother had rung me. You'd think a mother would have shown some tact in that situation even if she couldn't feel pity, but not her, oh no! *I suppose he got bored with your whining*, was all she could say, and with such satisfaction! That hurt more than the words. I put the phone down and fetched a cushion and opened the oven – even hung a blanket over the window, I got as far as that – but then I thought, that's the easy way, there's not meant to be ease in your life, my girl, you survive and put up with it, endure to the end. I'll survive this, George, don't you worry, better than you will, but that's what upsets me because when all's said and done, even if love's gone, there's always respect, and I want to respect you, George, don't take – don't take that from me . . .'

She was almost at an end now; her cadences changing as she moved through rage and self-pity to the pure luxury of poetic drama. George noted the slight hesitation in her last sentence. She had discarded the word 'away' because it would have spoiled the flow. And ended on a catch of breath. He waited until she began to weep softly – his cue – then put his arms round her. He said, 'My poor baby, you're tired. We'll talk in the morning.'

His mind raced with exhaustion as he settled as comfortably as he could in the chair; thoughts and memories succeeding each other with terrifying speed. His head was a filing cabinet and some alien madman had invaded it; was chucking the papers about . . .

No reason why he should not share Leila's bed except the embarrassment of Sally, asleep on the other. Leila would find that conclusive proof of his feelings if she thought about it when she woke in the morning.

As it was, of course.

Sam, waking, had said, 'Have you looked for them?' Cutting short his apologies. They were camping on a sheep-farm in the Welsh mountains. They walked down to the farm and found their bikes behind a low, dry-stone wall. Kids playing, probably: they knocked at the door of the house to ask for some milk and a couple of boys peered from an out-house, red-faced and giggling. 'Waste of time, wasn't it?' Sam said. 'All your breast-beating.'

Claire had small, pointed breasts with delicate veins. Breasts and lovely arms hidden beneath Sam's thick sweater. Hair the same colour as Sally's. She had grown it long again after that day at the Zoo. Sam had said, 'Pity, I liked it short.'

And George had felt guilty.

Sam said, 'Why does everything always have to be *your* fault? Seems to me just morally greedy.'

This was a much earlier occasion; the exact context forgotten. They had broken some rule at school and George had taken the blame. Owned up exultantly, piping-voiced. 'All my fault, sir.' He had wanted to do something for Sam; to express his love somehow. Sam had sensed this and disliked it. Or was afraid. He had called George a masochist – a word he had recently learned.

George objected. 'It was my fault. Really.' (*What* was? He couldn't remember. Only Sam's glowering face, his shamed look. And his own shame, understanding Sam's.) He had said, hiding behind generalities, 'You don't have to be a masochist to feel things are your fault. That if you'd done something differently something else wouldn't have happened.'

Like the hunter who went back in time, to a primæval forest, and changed the ecological development of the world because he trod on a butterfly. George had read this story in a science-fiction magazine when he was a boy and it had haunted him ever since like a popular tune. Or some small, distant guilt of the kind people are supposed to remember on their death-beds; not the real sins, the great betrayals, but the coppers they stole from their mother's purse, the moment they cheated, desperate to win some child's game . . .

His grandmother had cheated when she and Elspeth played cards. She said, 'If I don't cheat, dear, Elspeth always wins.' He had been a little shocked by her lack of shame and had said so to Elspeth. She said, 'Don't be a sodding prig, George. Only those people whose consciences are quite clear can afford to cheat. The bloody pure in heart.'

He hadn't understood Elspeth then. He did now. His grandmother could cheat at a game because there was no more to it than that: she had nothing deeper to reproach herself with that could cast a shadow over this peccadillo.

He thought – so clearly that it was like a sudden shout in his mind – no comfort there! And then – what had triggered *that* off? Was he looking for comfort? Not consciously, but in some sly, labyrinthine part of his mind. Trying to see himself, consolingly, as just a bluff, simple chap after all, one of Elspeth's 'bloody pure in heart'. George, the perpetual tourist, the innocent abroad, of whom the worst you could say was that he stumbled along in a state of clumsy absent-mindedness, only doing harm by default or mistake.

Treading, perhaps, on a butterfly . . .

Would she have got so involved with Zeynep if he had not dismissed her so summarily that foggy day on the Embankment? Dismissing her, she must have thought, because she was young, of no consequence. He had to do it, no option, but if he had not been so taken up with his own feelings he might have done it less brusquely, thought of some way to cushion her pride, make her feel she could still turn to him if she needed to . . .

He found himself laughing silently. Painfully cramped, on the verge of sleep, he thought – God, what folly! This wild paper-chase after first causes! Even with hindsight there was never a moment you could surely pin down among those millions of moments, each infinitely complex and all, to some all-seeing eye, clearly meshed into the future. He had remembered the butterfly story because it had appealed to his adolescent need to take himself seriously, to feel he could be effective in *some* way, but it was monstrous pride in a grown man to imagine he might have behaved differently at some selected second and so altered the face of the world. Not that this was a licence to trample about without thinking – only a warning not to look back too often at the muddy footprints behind you. A waste of time and dangerous, too; distracting attention from what lay ahead . . .

He had not expected to sleep. When he woke, he was astonished to find he had not only slept but felt rested. Only a slight ache in the small of his back. He stood up, cautiously stretching. Leila turned and muttered; then sighed and lay still. Sally was on her back, arms flung wide, lips parted, snoring a little. He looked down at them both with undiscriminating tenderness. No point in waking them until he had arranged something; booked Sally's flight, spoken to Omer. Dressing in the bathroom, he felt strong and competent and oddly excited. For once events were not passing him by. He told himself that it was frivolous to feel this. But it was not a response to a real situation. He was simply trusting that his life would run true to form; that what had happened last night had been no more than a bizarre and dreamlike diversion and nothing would come of it. Zeynep had met up with her associates, whoever they were, without further incident: whatever might happen to her eventually, there was no immediate danger to Sally. He left a note for Leila saying he would be back shortly, to wait for him and not worry, and went down to the lobby.

There was a message for him at the desk. Omer Kemal had called in at the hotel at seven o'clock. Would Mr Hare come to his office as soon as possible please? 'Why didn't you ring my room?' George asked, but the receptionist shrugged his shoulders, looking harassed and helpless. A large package tour had arrived; two coach loads of weary Americans besieging the desk with the dazed look of refugees from some cosmic disaster, or, outside the hotel, watching their luggage emerge from the bowels of the huge, panting buses.

A hand plucked George's arm; someone said, 'Are you our Leader?' A small, frail old woman with jewel-studded sun glasses and a trembling, dark-lipsticked mouth. He looked at her blankly but before he could answer she had moved on, calling out in a voice that seemed to break with despair, 'Martha! Martha! Are you watching the cases?'

George looked after her with a pitying, professional eye. Baggage neurosis was common among elderly women and could ruin a holiday. A good courier would have marked this one down early on and been on hand now, to console her. A taxi had pulled up in front of the buses and he got into it feeling distantly guilty because he had not helped her himself, spared a minute to reassure this stray lamb that she would not be beset by wolves outside the Istanbul Hilton. A small part, perhaps, but at least one he knew he played well . . .

Omer's office was noisy with traffic and the metallic *clank* of an ancient fan, lazily stirring the warm, heavy air. He looked up from his desk as his clerk showed George in. His plump face was unsmiling; his merry eyes shadowed and pouchy.

George said in a boisterous, defensive voice, 'You get to work early.'

Omer stood up, padded past him, shouted something at the clerk, closed the door. He said, 'The police sent a launch for me at four this morning. An inconvenient hour. I'm afraid Zeynep's in trouble.'

'I know.' Omer looked at him, frowning. George said quickly, 'Sally went to see Zeynep yesterday afternoon. They crossed over the ferry together. I picked Sally up on the other side.'

Omer sat down again heavily. He stared at George, yawning and rubbing his eyes.

George said, 'Sally didn't know what she was doing. She doesn't understand anything. She just wanted to help Zeynep. Do the police know she was with her?'

'I don't think so.' Omer sounded surprised as if this question hadn't occurred to him. Or wasn't important. He said, 'They've got Zeynep at headquarters. The security block. I saw her there. She wouldn't speak to me. They told me she'd killed this man.'

George said, 'It's unbelievable.'

'When I asked her about it, she just stared out of the window. Looked bored.'

George said, 'I thought she was gun-running.'

Omer spread out his hands, palm upwards, and grimaced.

George said, 'Has she told them anything?'

'Yes. Apparently. Her story is that this man was a friend.

An acquaintance, anyway. Someone she'd met at the university. He came to the flat the night before last and asked her for shelter. He said the Army were after him. She told him he could stay the rest of the night but he'd have to leave the next day. Then in the early hours of the morning he came into her room and tried to rape her. She says she shot him in self-defence. To defend her honour.'

'Could that be true?'

'I very much doubt it.'

'She just happened to have a gun handy? Do *they* believe that?'

'They've not questioned it yet. They're having her medically examined later this morning.'

'What for? She's not hurt? Oh – you mean a psychiatrist.'

Omer sighed. 'They're not concerned with her mental condition. Not that kind of refinement. They want to establish that she is really a virgin.'

'What's that got to do with it?'

'If she isn't, they'll naturally conclude she is lying. That since she is not a virtuous girl, she has no honour to defend.'

George laughed incredulously.

Omer looked at him. His face had sagged, like a sad monkey's. He said, 'This is Turkey, my friend. I suspect that whoever instructed her in this unlikely tale did not come from my country.'

'But it's preposterous!'

'To you, of course. I also find it somewhat absurd. But the people in control here are not sophisticated Europeans as they were under the old Ottoman Empire. Of course, if she is chaste, she may just get away with it.'

'With *murder*?'

'Oh, not altogether. But unless – or until – they turn up other evidence, they will at least treat her more gently.' His face contracted. There was sweat on his forehead.

George said, with horror, 'How *old* is she, Omer?'

'Nineteen.'

'Oh, God.' He thought – How stupid! What difference does it make?

Omer said, thoughtfully, 'She may be nearly twenty.'

'Have you told her parents?' He would have to ring Sam. Say Sally was coming home. Explain something.

Omer said, 'I hope Nili will have got hold of them by now.'

'Do they know who the man is?'

'They told me he's not been identified yet. So he's not a known terrorist. Which may be why they're proceeding so cautiously.'

George said, 'She didn't kill him. What she told Sally was, he'd disobeyed some order, that they'd shot him, I suppose in your flat – maybe she'd invited him there, I don't know – and she'd been told to dispose of the body.' He played these sentences back in his head and listened, amazed. He said, 'It sounds senseless.'

'No.' Omer was fiddling with a pencil, tapping it on the desk. 'It has exactly the right ring of absurdity.'

'So pointless.'

'Yes.'

George walked up and down the room; looked out of the window. Movement made him sweat; his shirt stuck to his back. He said, 'It's hotter than ever today, isn't it? How do they get hold of these *children*? It's not as if she'd been brought up in Turkey, even. She's an American girl, for Christ's sake! She must have met someone. I know she went off to Berlin when she was supposed to be ski-ing with Sally. She said she was seeing her boyfriend. Sally covered up for her.'

Omer said, 'That's a pity.'

'I suppose he was one of them. A terrorist. God, it sounds melodramatic! But that must be how it happened. He infected her with this *idiocy*!'

'Possibly,' Omer said. 'It's not important now. What I meant was it's a pity Sally knows so much about it.'

'At least they won't question her. As long as they believe this rape story. By the time they change their minds, if they do, she'll be out of the country. I'll get her onto a plane as soon as I can.'

'I shouldn't do that,' Omer said.

'Why ever not?'

Omer said, patiently, 'My dear friend, they'll be watching the airport. Whatever they're pretending to believe at this moment, they're taking precautions. They've already impounded my passport. And Sally has been staying with me. Another foreign girl I appear to be sheltering! If she seems to be leaving in rather a hurry they may want to know why. I think that is not a risk we should take.' He laughed, without humour. 'She might answer them truthfully.'

George closed his eyes. Wild ideas chased through his mind. He could say she was ill. Drug her. Bribe a doctor. Sally carried on to the plane, wrapped in a blanket . . . He breathed deeply and looked at Omer. He said, angrily, 'What do you suggest, then?'

Omer tapped with his pencil. 'If Sally knew nothing – really nothing – what would you do? I'm in a spot of trouble, but nothing that can affect her, and you're an old friend of her father's. It seems a pity to spoil the child's holiday, so as you're here, with your wife, you take her away with you. To Ankara, to visit the Hittite Museum. Or somewhere like Bursa, say. An interesting old spa and a most pleasant drive. What could look more natural?'

'And suppose Zeynep tells them that Sally had helped her? They may make her talk . . .' He stopped; forced himself to think what this meant. He said, 'I'm sorry, Omer.'

Omer nodded.

'I have to think about Sally.'

'Of course. I am deeply ashamed I have not taken better care of her.'

'If there was anything one could do for Zeynep . . .'

Omer said, 'We must hope that if Zeynep does tell them the truth, they will see that Sally is not really implicated. Or not in any serious way. They're not fools. Their job is to round up urban guerillas, not foolish young girls. If Sally behaves from now on as if she were totally innocent, I think they'll be glad to ignore her.'

'You can't be sure of that.'

'No. They're not always predictable.'

'But it's the best chance we've got?' George swallowed; the back of his throat seemed to have closed up. 'There is just one other thing. Not my question, but Sally's. She'd want me to ask it. Would it help Zeynep if she came forward, told the little she knew? That she'd been exploited . . .'

'No one can help Zeynep now,' Omer said.

Chapter 9

'It is known as Green Bursa,' Mary Bone said. 'There are supposed to be twenty-eight shades of green in the country around it. Bursa was once rather beautiful with a great many old wooden houses like those on Prince's Island but it is now just an industrial town and the spa is in one of its suburbs. The famous marble bath was built by Atatürk under the dome of a Turkish *hamam*. The water is hot and pleasant though I doubt whether it has all the curative properties some people claim for it. But you should enjoy swimming in the bath and looking round the town. You will notice the enormous number of doctors – one wonders how they all make a living – and quite a few veiled women, though of course the veil is illegal now. You mustn't miss the Green Mosque and you must drive up Uludağ, the Great Mountain. There are wolves and bear in its forests though I'm afraid the only wild animal you are likely to see will be a mothy old bruin tied up outside a tourist café. Turks are not over kind to their animals. The last time Arthur and I were here, we spoke to the café owner and persuaded him to put the poor creature on a slightly longer chain . . .'

She could have been conducting a Women's Institute outing. George sat beside her in the front of the car, grateful for the calm flow of her informative monologue and her large, calm hands on the wheel. When he had telephoned to say they were leaving for Bursa, she had offered to drive them at once and he had accepted with a relief that was more, he realized now, than the obvious comfort of having a guide who spoke Turkish, could read newspapers, interpret the news on the radio. She could only stay in Bursa for one night but he was wearily glad, at this moment, not to be alone with Sally and Leila. He felt the threat of their presence like two unexploded bombs in the back of the car. They had listened in silence while he told them what had happened to Zeynep; even when he had finished they had barely responded. Sally had wept, but in a soft, listless way that suggested resignation rather than fear, and although Leila had said, 'For God's sake, why didn't you tell me all this last night?' her implied resentment had been perfunctory, a mere matter of form. She had packed for the journey with unexcited efficiency, as if she found this fantastic situation perfectly normal. As perhaps it was, George had thought: for much of the world it is order and peace that is the abnormal state of affairs. But he had not expected Leila to feel this and, watching her, he began to dread her apparent acceptance as much as Sally's stunned, docile look. Shock had delayed their reactions but it was bound to come soon . . .

Mary Bone said, 'It is a moral tale, really. The man did what we asked and lengthened the chain but with one unfortunate result. A German visitor tried to take a close-up of the bear and got mauled in the process. Though not badly, I'm glad to say.'

Sally began to laugh. She threw herself about in the back of the car, clutching her stomach and braying with wide open mouth like a donkey. She tossed her head backwards and forwards. Not hysteria but a deliberate performance. Overacting like mad.

George said, with distaste, 'Please don't be so stupid, Sally.' She stopped at once and looked at him with such pain that he felt ashamed. He said, 'Really, you know, it wasn't so funny.'

She was looking at least ten years older. There was a line between her brows he had not seen before. She said humbly, 'I'm sorry. I didn't mean to be silly. But I don't know what to say. I don't know how I feel. I don't even know how to behave.'

This was true for him too, George acknowledged. The really unexpected happens so seldom that few of us know how to deal with it. We all move, for most of the time, in a small circle of known possibilities to which we have learned the responses. Outside this circle lies chaos; a dark land without guide-lines.

He tried to explain this to Sally, to comfort her. They left Mary and Leila at the hotel and walked through the town. They sat at a pavement café beneath flowering linden trees and drank small cups of thick, bitter coffee. The air smelt of blossom. He said, 'It's a matter of conditioning. What you're used to, as they say. If Zeynep had been badly hurt in a car-crash or picked up for shop-lifting or drugs, you'd be shocked of course, but in a much less disturbing way. You'd be less disorientated, even if she was the first person you knew this had happened to. The same way, if you were a Turkish girl, you wouldn't find this so unbelievable. Terrible, yes – but I think you'd accept it more easily. As an Indian, say, might accept a famine as a fact of life, not just something to be read about in the papers.'

He thought – What bland rubbish! Dead men were not found in trunks every day, even in Turkey. But she hadn't been listening.

She said, 'I'm ashamed. A woman once came to our house and said she'd been to Egypt and hadn't enjoyed her holiday because of the beggars. My parents laughed when she'd gone but it wasn't so stupid, only the way that she put it. I know how she felt because I feel it now. As if I'd lived all my life at other people's expense. On their *backs*. I despise myself. I've been so *pig-ignorant*.'

'That's not your fault. Don't feel guilty.'

She looked at him. Her face was immobile. The little line between her brows might have been carved there. She said carefully, 'When I try to think about Zeynep, I *can't* think. My mind freezes up. I can't imagine what's happening to her, or what's going to happen. But I don't feel guilty about her. Was that what you were expecting me to feel? That I wish I'd stayed with her, that whatever she'd done it would be the right thing for *me* to do because she's my friend?'

He nodded and she smiled. The smile smoothed her face out. Even her voice sounded younger. 'Perhaps I ought to think that but I don't. What I feel is something much vaguer. I don't know how to explain it. Yes, I do! It's as if I'd lived all my life in a palace with gold doors and jewelled walls and beautiful pictures that I thought were windows, and suddenly someone had opened one of those gold doors onto oh, I don't know – *howling darkness* – and I'm standing there, looking out, scared to death, and knowing she's out there somewhere and I could be, too, if I took one more step . . .'

He reached across the table and took her hand. He said, 'I'm here to hold on to. Try not to be frightened.'

She looked down at their linked hands and frowned slightly. Had this gesture embarrassed her? Wondering if it had, embarrassed *him*. He had only intended to comfort her but now he felt like a licentious bastard who had used this pretext to grab hold of the girl. But to withdraw his hand seemed too obvious. He compromised by loosening his fingers.

She gave a sudden, shy laugh that made his heart lurch. But all she said was, 'That was dreadfully over-dramatic, wasn't it? Palaces and gold doors! I mean, I did feel something like that but I sort of dressed it up, didn't I? And made it less real somehow.'

'Putting things into words does that sometimes.'

She looked at him sadly. Her eyes were luminous. 'But it's dreadful the way it takes the sting out! Oh, I'm putting *that* badly. What I mean is, talking about it has made me feel it's all really quite bearable! Just something that's happened that I'm going to file away in my mind. Not to forget about, I don't mean that, but something that's over and done with.'

'I hope it is for you.'

'I don't care about me! Oh, that's silly, of course I do, I'm not stupid. But I meant *Zeynep*. All I can see is her getting into that bus and me watching her go. That's the last thing. *The end*. It's as if I'd typed a last sentence and drawn a thick black line underneath it.'

She began to shake. He squeezed her hand. He was aching with love.

She wailed, 'There I go again! Verbalizing! And half enjoying it in a way because I'm here with you and you're *listening* to me, and tucked away in the back of my mind I can't help thinking that we wouldn't be together like this if this frightful thing hadn't happened! I know I can't *help* thinking that but I hate myself for it. And I hate myself for hating myself because it means I'm thinking about me instead of about her which I ought to be doing and *can't*. Oh George, help me, please. Am I going mad?'

'No. No, my darling, you're not.' He thought – I should be ashamed to be feeling so happy! He said, 'It's all caught up with you suddenly. That's all. A natural reaction. Talk as much as you like. Cry if you want.'

She said, 'I can't cry.'

Leila said, 'I must say she's taking it surprisingly calmly. I wish I could. But then I've always been sensitive.'

George looked at her. She seemed a total stranger, sitting on the edge of the round, marble bath in her bathing costume and a cap made to look like a curly, blonde wig, her pretty, dimpled legs in the hot, murky water. The high *hamam* dome above them was streaked with green, either slime or algae, and the evening sun slanted through symmetrically placed holes like small searchlight beams. Opposite them, an immensely fat man sat motionless under the hot jets of a fountain, shoulders hunched, legs crossed, like a Buddha. Mary and Sally were in the bath; Mary swimming with slow, stately strokes, Sally floating on her back, her pale, mermaid's hair streaking the water.

He said, 'She can't go on crying woe. None of us can.'

'I shan't be able to eat a thing tonight!' Leila lifted her chin defiantly as if she had just made a momentous decision he was likely to dispute. 'Or sleep, either. Did you know there was no air-conditioning in the old part of the hotel where our rooms are? It's scandalous in this frightful heat. Of course, once I'd unpacked, I discovered there was a new modern annexe just over the road! But although Mary asked when I told her, they didn't seem over-willing to move us. Laziness, of course – a bit further to carry the bags! What they *said* was, it wasn't officially opened yet, but Mary thinks that if we really insist they won't fuss too much about that. I'm afraid she thought *I* was fussing. She didn't actually say so but by saying nothing she made me feel small. I don't want to fuss. I suppose it depends on how long we're likely to stay here.'

'Mary will book Sally's plane as soon as it seems we can get her away without incident. Arthur should be able to gauge that. He has various contacts.'

She said, disapprovingly, 'It all seems so unnecessary. So melodramatic!'

'Just cautious.'

'I mean, behaving as if she had done something criminal.'

'It might seem to them that she had.'

'But that's nonsense. An English girl of her age. They'd only have to take one look at her!'

'I'm afraid they might not see what we see.'

Sally had got out of the pool and was standing beside one of the marble basins that surrounded it, using a pink plastic dish to sluice herself with cold water. The eyes of the fat Buddha under the fountain had swivelled to watch her. She threw back her head and poured water over her upturned face, gasping with pleasure. She called out to them, 'Oh, it's marvellous.'

George smiled.

Leila said, 'I'm trying hard to be sensible, George. But it seems so unreal. Particularly here, in this extraordinary bath.'

While she spoke, she was looking at Sally. George saw her straighten her back and pull in her stomach muscles. The wig-like bathing cap was creasing the loose skin at the side of her eyes. He said, with compunction, 'It's always hard to do nothing. But there could be worse places, couldn't there? The spa water is supposed to be good for rheumatism. The metals in it, or something. Or perhaps only the heat. It might help that pain in your shoulder.'

'Except that I haven't got it at this moment, of course.'

'Pity.' He laughed at her until she smiled back reluctantly. He said, 'We'll move our room before dinner. There's no reason why you should have even one sleepless night.'

The original hotel had been built at the same time as the great bath and had the same solid, if decaying, elegance. The modern annexe was brightly painted but shoddier. 'Built of matchboxes,' Leila cried. 'It's disgraceful when you think of the money they charge. Soak the poor tourist, that's always the thing! If there was anyone in the next room, you'd hear every sound.'

'Do you want to move back?'

'No. At least the air-conditioning works. I thought I was going to pass out at supper, the heat was so dreadful. You'd think it would get a bit cooler at night, wouldn't you? But it seemed hotter than ever.'

'Brewing up for a storm, perhaps. It's cool enough here, isn't it? In the room. Try and relax. Rest. You'll feel better soon. Or would you like to go back to the bath? That might help you to sleep. They don't close until midnight.'

She lay on her bed, on her back, staring up at the ceiling. She said without emotion, 'You don't know how I feel.'

He thought perhaps he had sounded perfunctory. He said, 'You're simply tired, aren't you? It's hardly surprising.'

She turned her head and looked at him steadily. Then she said, 'I'm a bore. I bore myself. Can you understand that? I have to live with this bore that's myself and it's a life-sentence. A prison. I wish I could escape but I can't. I can't enjoy life. I can't look forward as you do.'

She wasn't accusing him, he realized with surprise. There was a note in her voice, a kind of sad, tranquil acceptance, he thought he had not heard before. He said cautiously, 'I suppose I do enjoy life. Not always, of course. Not perhaps at this moment. But on the whole, yes.'

'Because you see joy ahead. Not any specific thing, just an infinite number of possibilities. In front of me, there's only a narrowing tunnel.'

'You're wary, that's all. You see there's likely to be a hitch in most things.' He tried to laugh. 'A more practical approach, really.'

'I used to explain it like that. Safer not to be trustful. But it isn't so simple. What's wrong with me, this staleness I feel, isn't just distrust or pessimism or some kind of middle-aged hormonal disturbance but some vital thing missing. I've learned that, living with you.'

Amazingly, she was smiling. He crinkled his eyes up at the corners and said, 'Hey! Steady on! What have I done?'

'Nothing wrong. You've been good to me, George. But you have a hopeful heart and I haven't. I don't mean you never expect the worst to happen, you're not that sort of fool. But whatever you say or believe, however you hedge it about, you know in your heart that if the worst does ever come you'll somehow live through it, make something out of it. Go on – *travelling*. And that's not just a lucky gift, a pleasant extra, as I used to think before I met you. It's something you can't live without, or not in any meaningful way. Every day we're together I see what's lacking in me, why I've gone as far as I'll ever go on the road, and it's like looking, not just at my own failure, but at my own *death*. You've made me see I have a fatal disease.'

She said all this very calmly, looking at him with huge eyes and smiling. He was astonished; almost afraid. She wasn't on stage at this moment, or if she was, this was a better performance than she had ever put on before. He thought – Perhaps she means it, this time! But he was less affected than he would have been by a piece of good theatre. He felt nothing for her at all.

He said, 'You *are* tired.'

She looked at him and sighed.

He said, 'When something happens like this, some crisis or other when everything turns topsy-turvy, you start to question all sorts of things. As you do sometimes when you wake up in the night. You don't necessarily come up with the answers.'

She was smiling again. 'I expect you're right. I'll feel differently in the morning.'

'Yes. Try and sleep now. We'll talk if you like but I really think you need sleep more than anything.'

She closed her eyes and lay on her back, legs and arms spread wide. He thought, as he closed the door, that she looked like a starfish left behind on a dry rock by the tide.

And then, as he crossed the road from the annexe to the hotel – Perhaps she will kill herself.

The ante-room to the bath was lit by fluorescent tubes speckled with fly dirts. There were low tables and brown, plastic-covered armchairs, and a machine that dispensed sweet, bottled fruit-drinks. The air smelt of seaweed.

Mary Bone was talking to Sally. 'The Army in Turkey could be called the school of the nation. Turks are very egalitarian and all young men do their military service. Peasants learn to read and write – in the case of some of them, Kurds for example, they even have to be taught Turkish! – and all new recruits are mixed up so that they meet others from different geographical areas. This means that the Army is a powerfully cohesive force, much respected at all levels of society. But the country is a democracy and the force's chiefs respect *that*. They have been impatient, sometimes, with the inefficiency of the democratic process and they have certainly over-reacted to the terrorist movement, but basically they are not interested in permanent power. They are sophisticated enough to want to avoid a Latin-American situation, where the military is drawn deeper and deeper into the day to day administration of the country, which might lead to endless coups and counter-coups. I am quite sure that once this present crisis is over they will withdraw from political intervention and there will be elections.'

If the last bomb fell, George thought, the first sound to arise in the dusty air would be that gentle, clear, didactic voice, explaining that the wreckage would be tidied up soon. He said, 'Sally looks tired.'

179

She shook her head gallantly. 'I did ask. I wanted to understand . . .'

Mary said, 'One has to put the situation into historical perspective, dear. It is important to see the general picture. To get some idea of the complicated issues involved.'

George wondered why she should have spoken like this, with the droning repetition of someone reading from a badly written, official document. Mary could be long winded but she was usually precise. He said, 'It's late, Mary.'

Sally frowned at him. 'I really was interested.' But her eyes were drifting with sleep. She yawned and said, 'I'm sorry. I suppose it's the bath. That lovely, hot water.'

'You were in a long time,' Mary said.

She nodded, still yawning, then pushed back the sleeve of her white, towelling robe. 'My skin's gone slippery. It's the water. Feel.' She extended one glossy arm. George touched it gently.

She said, 'I swam under the water. It booms in your ears like the sea in a cave. I kept thinking, I wish I could swim with no clothes on.'

Mary said, 'In a real Turkish *hamam* you could. The sexes are segregated. But it can be managed here, too. The last time Arthur and I came, we tipped the attendant and asked him to let no one else in. Of course we got up very early in the morning, at a time when other people were unlikely to be using the bath. I think we inconvenienced no one.'

George thought of his two old friends swimming; of their large, white, lumbering bodies. Plump buttocks like moons in the dark, steely water. Of Sally, naked. Then of Claire.

He said, 'Do you know that story about your mother, Sally?'

Spoilt, stubborn, lovely Claire, marching into her parents' cocktail party in Nairobi, wearing only a string of pearls her father had given her.

Sally was looking puzzled. She had never heard this. When George told her she laughed, but not altogether approvingly. 'It was a bit bitchy, really. To embarrass people like that.'

'She was only fourteen. She didn't see why she should be left out of a party.'

Sally didn't reply at once. She chewed the skin at the side of her thumb and blinked rapidly. Then she shook her head as if to dismiss some uncomfortable thought that had come to her and said, 'I suppose we all do stupid things when we're young.'

Sally's room was on the top floor. Mary and George walked with her as far as the lift. She kissed them both very affectionately. As the lift creaked upwards, Mary said, 'You will have to tell her tomorrow that Zeynep is dead.'

She had spoken so softly and flatly that for a moment George wondered if he had really heard her say this.

He said, '*What*?'

She nodded. Her eyelids flickered and her large hand fumbled with the collar of her white robe. She said, 'Arthur telephoned while you were changing your room. He had dinner with the Chief of Police this evening. It will be in the papers tomorrow.'

He said, 'Oh, Christ. How? What happened?'

'She threw herself out of the window. They took her to hospital but she died before they got there. Her back was broken.'

He swallowed. He couldn't think what to say. He cleared his throat unnecessarily. Mary was looking at him. He had to say something. He said, 'Weren't they watching her?'

'Not carefully enough, obviously. Arthur didn't say how it happened.'

'They let her jump out of the *window*?'

She said dryly, 'The windows in the security block are

usually kept closed against just this eventuality. I suppose it was simply so unbearably hot. And perhaps they thought there was no danger since her parents were coming. I don't know. Accidents happen.'

'Had she told them anything? Apart from that nonsense about being raped?'

'Arthur said, at the time it happened they were still waiting for the doctor's report. I doubt if they would have questioned her further until they had that. They are very legalistic.'

He thought – Sally is safe now! And then, shocked by the enormous relief flooding through him, 'God, how terrible. That poor girl!'

'Some people might think she was lucky. There are worse things than a quick death.'

He looked at her. At this kindly English woman standing in a drably lit hotel corridor far from home and calmly saying these incredible sentences. He said, angrily, 'Tell me, Mary. Can you really fit this into an historical perspective?'

She smiled at him sadly.

He said, 'Oh, I'm sorry. You were only trying to avoid telling Sally tonight. I know that.'

There were tears in her pale eyes but she made no attempt to wipe them away. She would not wish to call attention to her own feelings in this situation. She said, 'I am almost a stranger to her and she's very young. I thought it would be best if she heard it from someone she knows well. Someone who loves her.'

He looked at her uneasily but she was incapable of innuendo; had meant nothing beyond this simple statement. It would be natural for George to love his best friend's child, after all. She said, 'She's a good girl. Very easy to love.'

George thought – Perhaps Leila is dead, too! Bodies strewn all over the stage, like the last act of *Hamlet*. An empty bottle of Nembutal by her bed. This had been in his mind earlier. Why had he done nothing about it? Perhaps he didn't believe it. Or had hoped it would happen?

His grandmother would have said it was some kind of fore-knowledge. A smell of death in the air like the electrical tension before a storm. Only Zeynep, not Leila.

She was sleeping. Snoring gently, on her back, with one knee lifted. A tender, blue vein snaked down the inside of one thigh. The air-conditioner hummed unevenly. She had not taken even one sleeping pill: there was a full bottle, untouched, in her wash-bag. Although these pills had been prescribed for her, she was unwilling to take them because she had read that they were addictive. He thought – She will go on living with her fatal disease. She will tell me about her symptoms and I will go on listening. The map of our lives laid down for us. A long road ahead with no turnings.

He got into bed and turned out the light. Lay in the dark and thought – At least it's straightforward now. Tomorrow I will tell Sally her friend is dead. Comfort her if I can. We will drive back with Mary. I will telephone Sam and put Sally on a plane. Send her safe home to her father.

He woke at six. Leila was sleeping. When he got up she muttered and tossed and opened her eyes. He said, 'Go back to sleep. It's still early. I'm going to swim.'

She smiled drowsily. 'Perhaps I'll come later.'

He put his towelling-robe on over his trunks and went down in the lift. Outside the annexe the heat was almost palpable: crossing the road, his limbs felt heavy and slow as if he were moving through water. The sky was cloudlessly blue; solid as a painted canopy over his head.

In the hotel lobby, the desk clerk was asleep with his mouth open. George went down to the bath and found the ante-room empty although the attendant was already on duty:

he could hear the swish of a broom from the changing rooms at the end.

He went through the doors into the domed, marble bath. Sally was standing in the water with her back to him, moving her arms in a slow, circular, sensuous movement that sent little dark waves rippling over her shoulders. He said, 'Sally,' and she turned quickly. With an odd, guilty look. He said, 'You're up early.'

'I did what Mary said. Got up early and tipped the attendant. Not enough, apparently.'

For a second he didn't understand what she meant. Then he said, 'Oh. Oh, yes. I see.'

'Well, you can't *actually*. The water's so murky.'

'Yes. Yes, it is. Shall I go away?'

She shook her head, laughing at him.

He hesitated. He thought – How ridiculous! He took off his robe and slid into the pool. He said, conversationally, 'It doesn't seem as hot as it did yesterday. Perhaps because it's so hot outside.'

'I couldn't sleep. Did you?'

'Quite well.'

'Did Leila?'

'I think so.'

Her mouth trembled with laughter. She said, 'What other polite things can we say to each other?'

He said, 'Someone else might have come in. What would you have done?'

'Stayed in the water until they went, I suppose.'

'Or that bloke outside might have made a pass at you. Thought you'd invited him!'

'I didn't say I was going to swim naked. Just that I wanted to swim on my own. He didn't seem to think that particularly odd. Other people must ask him occasionally. Arthur and Mary did.'

'A married couple are in a different position from a girl on her own.'

She giggled, 'Don't be so prim, George.'

He said indignantly, 'I'm not prim!' And thought – I must stop this! He had to tell her Zeynep was dead. That her friend had thrown herself out of a window and broken her back. But he couldn't tell her now. Not while she had no clothes on. He couldn't analyse this categorical feeling. He thought – This is quite the silliest situation I have ever been in.

She said, 'George . . .'

She was swimming close to him now. Her breasts bobbed on the surface of the water like two buoyant pears, pale-tipped where the sun had not touched them.

He looked at her breasts; then at her face.

She laughed and brushed sleekly against him. Then rolled on her side.

He said, 'Sally!'

She laughed again, softly. He stood still and she turned in the water smooth and quick as a fish and slid her body past his, stroking him with her belly and thighs.

A curious tremor went through him. It was as if the floor of the bath had suddenly moved under his feet. He thought – Delight or dread? The earth shifting. He felt giddy. He shook his head and stepped back. Pleading with her. 'Stop it, Sally. Please.'

'Why?' She floated towards him, smiling. A fair girl in a dream. An enchantress.

He closed his eyes and said furiously, 'Because I love you, you silly, ignorant girl.'

No answer. She didn't touch him. He waited. Counted to ten, very slowly, then opened his eyes. She was standing a few yards away, watching him. Choppy little waves lapped her shoulders. She stammered, 'I'm sorry.'

She was out of his reach. He smiled at her carefully. He said, 'Don't be. Just forget I said that.'

'I don't want to.'

'Well. All right. Don't count it, then. Treat it as irrelevant.' What on earth did he mean? He said, 'This is such an odd place. This bath. The world spinning round and us here. At a fixed point, a still centre, where we can do and say what we like. But that's an illusion. Out of context, you see.'

She didn't reply. She put her arms up and pushed her wet hair back. Her expression was scornful. She looked as if she were facing into a gale. A ship's figurehead, riding black water.

He felt unutterably foolish. He said 'Listen. I've got something to tell you. Someone may come in any moment. Please get out now and put something on.'

He didn't look at her again. He turned on to his back and lay floating, eyes fixed on the high dome above. The holes in the dome, through which the sun should be shining, were dark.

His mind registered this curious fact but not its significance. He was thinking of Sally.

She shouted, 'George . . .'

She was standing by the fountain, one hand against the wall, her head thrown back, staring up. She had fastened her wet hair in a topknot so that when he called back to her and she turned towards him, he recognized her at once; absolutely. Saw, in that vividly remembered gesture, in the way her head was set on the unbroken sweep of her naked spine as she looked down at him, exactly who she was; without doubt, without question. Without, even, surprise . . .

Recognition, not revelation. He had known this for so long and hidden it from himself for so many, convoluted, human reasons. Guilt at first, naturally. He had needed this living evidence that he had betrayed Sam. And fear of appearing ridiculous. He might act the fool but that was a self-protective game: you shout loudest what you fear most. Perhaps, in the end, that was the real truth of it. He had preferred to shelter behind the lie of this oldest tabu, rather than commit himself to his folly; jump with both feet into the deep end of an absurd, hopeless love . . .

Had Claire understood how he felt? Probably not. She had, after all, tried to tell him the truth. Had dropped hints and clues – not her fault he'd ignored them. She couldn't tell him outright; was too kind. How could she admit that she'd tricked him; had been bored at Oxford, with Sam playing rugger? Even if it had not been as simple as that – few things were – could she have said, once she knew, was quite *sure* as at some point she must have been, sorry, old chap, not your child, but Sam's? He got there first, after all. Oh, she could, if she'd wanted to: she was kind, but direct. Why not, then? Leila would say – *had* said when he told her about poor old Barnet – that a woman might enjoy the sense of conspiracy, would like to keep a man tied to her, sharing the secret. But Leila always took the low view. Claire wasn't like that. Unless she had loved him, been glad there was this bond between them? No, that was absurd. More likely, she felt guilty too. As he did. Not putting the record straight was her way of atoning . . .

Not that it mattered. How could it matter how this had happened? Life turns on such stupidities. His life, anyway. He laughed aloud as he got out of the bath.

Sally said, 'George . . .'

He ran to her. She held out her hand and he took it. He said, 'D'you know who you look like? Sam's mother!'

She stared at him. 'I know *that*. Only she had dark hair.

For God's sake!' She clutched his hand. 'George. The wall *moved!'*

He stood still. He felt nothing. Her wet body glimmered beside him. She said, 'Look . . .'

He looked where she pointed. A grey, steely light filtered through the holes in the dome. Like the light in a cave.

He said, 'The sun's gone.'

She was pressing against him. Her warm, silky body. A phrase came into his head. *It gets the old pecker up*. The manager at the supermarket who was turned on by veiled women. George thought – How grotesque! He wondered where he had taken his wife and his daughters for this year's summer holiday.

Sally said, 'Not just that . . .'

As they watched, the holes in the dome shifted slightly; moved, very slowly, closer together, then apart again. As if the whole structure were breathing. He could feel the tremor now, under his feet. The faint shudder of a boat moving over calm water.

He said, 'It's an earthquake.'

She looked at him wonderingly. He said, 'Stay where you are.'

His robe lay on a marble bench close to the fountain. He kept his back to her while he put it on, for concealment. He thought – At a time like this! Lord, how stupid.

She had put on her own gown. She looked at him trustingly. He said, 'I thought I felt something earlier. When we were in the pool. Don't be frightened.'

She shook her head. He said, 'There's my brave girl.'

She said, 'The water's gone dark. Will the roof come down on us?'

She spoke with astonishing calm. He thought – The young can face death. He said, 'This could be a good place. A *hamam*.'

He wondered if this were true. The old *hamams* were built much lower than this. But perhaps it wasn't the height that preserved them but the way they were built. He said, 'It's something to do with the curve of the dome. The stresses and strains. I'm afraid I don't understand it.'

She giggled. 'Mary would tell you.' Then looked horrified.

He said, 'I expect she's alright. It didn't seem too bad in here.'

'We can't tell, can we?' She gasped. 'Suppose she tried to come in and the man outside stopped her?'

'He didn't stop me. Don't worry. I'll go and see.'

Leila had said she was coming.

He said, 'You'd better stay. You'll be safer. I'll come back for you.'

'No.'

'*Yes*. Please, my darling.'

She said, 'Don't be a fool, George.'

The ante-room was empty. As they ran up the stairs there was another vibration but very slight; no more than the trains had made, passing the bottom of his grandmother's garden when he was a boy, lying in bed and feeling the iron frame shake. The glass in the hotel lobby was shattered; chalky dust filled the air. People, some in their night-clothes, stood beneath the shelter of the staircase, huddled together. A man was sweeping up glass. A child cried.

Outside, the sky was blue again, though seen through a floating, pink haze. The sun, a liquid, crimson ball, hung low. George looked at the sun. He should not have been able to see it from here, not at this time of day. The new annexe on the other side of the road shut out the eastern light.

Glass tinkled under his feet. In the street a donkey

clattered past, a man bouncing on its back. Someone was shouting somewhere. Dogs howled in the valley.

The main hotel stood but the annexe had crumbled into rubble and dust. One wall remained, bits of floor still attached; halfway up, a lavatory basin hung, swaying gently. George watched it fall, breaking neatly in two, both halves bouncing. Silence fell. Nothing moved. The dogs had stopped barking. Then a strange, gentle, sighing and whispering as bricks and dust settled.

The man who had been sweeping up glass touched George's arm. The hotel-manager; an elegantly dressed man in a dark suit, covered in dust like a miller. He said, 'Mr Hare, was your wife with you?'

George shook his head.

'The wall may come down. When we are sure it is safe, we will look for her. I think she was the only guest in the annexe.' He stopped. He said, 'I am sorry.'

George nodded.

The manager said, 'I have sent the girl to stand under the stair with the others. I think it is finished now, but it is best to take care.'

George said, 'Yes.'

The manager coughed, then apologized. 'The dust,' he said.

George looked at the ruin. No one could be alive there. He thought – But she may be! Miracles happened. People survived; were found buried, but breathing. He would behave as if it were possible. In a minute he would run forward, shouting her name, tearing at bricks and planks with his bare hands, praying to find her.

He saw himself doing these things, his body performing these functions, but his mind froze, unbelieving . . .

. . . and remembering a story. A tale he and Sam had been told long ago by an English settler one night in Nairobi. A farmer from the Rift Valley getting drunk in a bar, and telling two young men, playing at soldiers in Kenya, what had happened to him during the Mau Mau uprising. During the rains. His car had bogged down in a patch of mud in a village up country. He had asked for help, not expecting trouble – there had been none, so far, in this district – but the villagers had been paid for pulling vehicles through the mud all the morning and were drunk on the proceeds. They dragged him out of his car, turned it over, and tied him up, arms to his sides, legs together. This done, they seemed uncertain what to do next and left him, standing in the hot sun outside the small general store. They surrounded him, jeering. He understood, slowly, that they were waiting for someone to come, some local elder, or political leader, and that when this man came they would kill him. He was dizzy, sick with fear and the sun beating down, and after a while the shopkeeper, a timid-eyed Indian, brought a chair and placed it beside him.

The villagers fell silent at once, watching him, and he knew that if he sat down they would knock him off the chair and beat him, perhaps even to death. But not to acknowledge the Indian's kindness seemed, quite simply, impossible, and it was at this point that fear left him completely; and not only fear, but all feeling beyond a certain chilled curiosity. It was, he said, as if he had been removed from his body and was watching himself from a distance: a middle-aged, English farmer, tied up like a parcel and obeying an ingrained, nursery rule of politeness even though it might mean his own death.

He sat down and they knocked the chair from beneath him as he had known that they would. But although they kicked him as he lay on the ground, they only hurt him a little, as if they had grown bored or uneasy, and when evening came and whoever they were waiting for had not come – or perhaps he had only imagined they were waiting for some-one – they righted his car and untied him.

George thought – I am remembering this story now because nothing happened, after all, in the end – and it seemed, sud-denly, that he saw himself plain at last. Observing himself from afar, and observing himself observing himself, as in an infinite series of mirrors; George Hare, standing in the shattered doorway of an hotel in Turkey, remembering an old story for the easy comfort of its anti-climax and wonder-ing if he might fit it into his own repertoire, as he would fit this one day, telling how he had stood here, in a white towell-ing robe, waiting for a wall to come down, for the moment when he would act, run forward, tear at the rubble, shout his wife's name, feel grief or joy, and while he was waiting, remembering a story he had once heard a man tell, a man whose name he couldn't remember . . .

A character in fiction, summing up his life in an anecdote. He thought of himself this way, to understand himself better, place himself in all this confusion, in this terrible, beautiful world. To try to make sense of his part in it.

But that wasn't possible. Or not for him, anyway. All he could reasonably ask, for himself, was that he would go on doing as well as he could what he had to do, even if the real action always seemed to him somewhere else, not where he was; his place on the fringe of it, anxiously but hopefully watching. George of the hopeful heart. Surviving to tell the tale.

Dogs were barking again in the valley. A cock crowed. The manager said, 'I think the wall will stand safe, Mr Hare,' and George began running.